"Love Will Find a Way"

A Lesbian Romance

Christine L'Amour

Chapter One

Diana snatched a dirty rag from a stool and wiped it across her forehead. An entire day spent laboring under an old car trying to fix the damn thing had made her sweaty, exhausted, and hungry, but she still had a few hours to go. She patted the hood of the car and sat down on the stool, looking over the many papers on top of the desk in front of her. Plans, plans, finances, a lot of bills to pay.

Hm. If she paused the car now and went to work on old Jamie's motorcycle, she could be done with it in two days instead of three, and maybe he'd leave her a nice tip.

"Hey, girl. Have you eaten yet? It's already two in the afternoon."

Diana looked up. Jimmy was leaning against the door to the rickety stairs that led up to her apartment, a towel in his hands. His thick grey beard was streaked with tomato sauce. He was her best friend, this fat grandpa who'd stayed with them through everything, the accident, the debt, the new business.

"Hey, Jimmy," she said. "I haven't had *lunch*, but I've eaten some stuff."

"Stuff?"

She shrugged. He sent her an unimpressed look.

"There's some pasta here," he told her. He patted his belly, a bit anxious. "Look, Di… I won't be able to come visit for a couple of weeks after this. My kids want me to spend some time with them, then the wife wants to travel on the weekends—"

"Hey, Jimmy," Di interrupted. "You've got your family. You know it's all fine. You don't have to apologize. We'll see each other when you can come, okay? Besides, we can still call."

He frowned.

"None of that," he said. "You know you're family too. My son and my daughter are just annoyed that I come make food for you but not for them. Bah! I'd make it if they *needed* me to."

Diana sighed theatrically. "I do need you, Jimmy. I don't know how I'll live these couple of weeks without you."

He rolled his eyes, turned around, and made his way up the stairs, probably back to the kitchen. "Call your sister!" he shouted down. "Manny's been yelling at me about you not answering your damn phone, *again*."

She grumbled, but fished her phone out of her pocket. She had a bunch of missed calls and unread texts. Ooops. She dialed Manny's number.

"Hey, baby sis," she said. She put the phone between her cheek and her shoulder to free her hands. She shuffled papers around, organizing them in piles. "Sorry about the missed texts, I've been working on Jim's old Chevy again. I think I nailed it down, there's something wrong with the—"

"I cannot believe this," Manny interrupted. "Two years ago if *I* had done something like this you'd have skinned me, and now *you're* the one not answering your phone!"

"Two years ago, you were a seventeen-year old shrimp being bullied in high school, now you're a wonderful college girl out there conquering the world."

"So?"

"Are you complaining about me *not* being a mother hen? Because I can go back to doing that."

Manuela paused. Diana eyed the big pile of bills. She had to pay them sometime.

"I actually called to talk about my rent," Manuela said.

Diana groaned. "If that damned thing went up *again*, I swear to—"

"No, no! It's the same. It's just that Karen just told us she's moving in with her girlfriend soon—she should have told us *months* ago. But anyway, that means me and Angela will have to cover her third until we find someone else to come live here with us—"

"How long?" Diana interrupted. "You know I have your college savings. There's enough money for an ample time in there."

"Diana," Manuela said, exasperated, "I *told* you already to abolish the damn savings account. I'm here, *I'm working*, I have enough money—"

"Then why call, baby sis?" Diana said, unconvinced.

"Because if I didn't tell you and you found out later, you'd kill me," Manuela said dryly.

"… okay, that's true."

"I can handle myself. And how's the shop going, Di? I can't believe that old car is there *again*."

"It's all going well. So I'll transfer some of the funds to you later today, okay? I've a bunch of damn bills to pay anyway. "

"*Diana.*"

"You're my baby sister," Diana said. "I'll transfer the damn money. You work for yourself, get your money for your things, and *I'll pay for the college stuff.* You know I will."

"You want to expand your business but most of your damn money goes to me! It's not fucking fair. I'm working so I won't be as much of a damn burden—"

"You're not a damn burden."

Silence rang between them. The city was loud; cars honked outside and a cat mewed hungrily. Diana threw the rag over her shoulders toward the table and stood up. She better eat some damn pasta before she went to work on that motorcycle.

"That's not what I meant," Manny finally said. Di could picture her drooping down.

"If it's not what you meant, then don't say it." Diana made her way up the stairs. The tiny apartment smelled like Jimmy's home-made tomato sauce. Her mouth watered. "I'll send you the money."

"I'll spend it all on booze instead of rent."

"I trust you to do the right thing," Diana said, too serious to be joking.

Manny groaned.

"Fine! Go work on Jamie's car or whatever. Don't forget you're visiting in a few weeks."

"You think I'll forget? Is that what you think of me?"

Manny groaned again, loud and theatrical, and hung up the phone. Diana made her way to the kitchen.

***

It was pushing eleven p.m. when Diana sighed and finally let herself stand up. The bike would be there tomorrow and her whole body was shaking from the stiff positions she held the whole day and she wanted a shower more than anything right now. She carded a hand through her hair and pushed it back from her face and walked with rigid limbs to the front part of her garage.

It was more formal than her actual working place, just a little room with a desk, some chairs, some plants; a place her one employee Carl could meet costumers. Rain was beating against the windows upfront and—

Diana froze.

There was a woman standing tersely and close to the door, soaked to her *bones*. She was one of the most beautiful things Diana had ever seen—her skin was flushed pink and her hair in a tight bun was very dark. Her eyes were dark as night. There were lines carved around her face, marking tiredness that spoke of years, but still she wore it well. She was tall and thin as a beanpole, swallowed by a tan coat.

She was strangely familiar. Something about those eyes, she thought, or maybe those full lips.

Diana managed to unstick her feet from the floor and walked up to the desk. What was this? A customer? This woman didn't seem like the kind of person who'd go fix her car in a hole-in-the-wall place like Di's. Maybe she was lost.

"We're closed," Di said, a bit confused. "It's almost eleven."

"Apologies," the woman said stiffly. Strangely, she didn't move one inch from where she stood, not even to walk toward Di, though she squinted at her. It was kind of adorable, Di thought. "The sign on the door says you're open. I was just looking for somewhere to wait for the rain to pass. Nothing else is open right now."

Diana's eyes flitted away to the front windows. The rain was heavy and it wouldn't stop for a long time. She looked back at the woman. Water dripped from her to Di's floor.

"Well," Di said. "Make yourself at home. How about I bring you some towels? There's no heater here, but there's one back at the garage if you want to try and dry up a bit."

"Thank you," she said. "I wouldn't want to bother. I would appreciate a towel, however."

"Cool."

Diana walked out to the garage and then up to her apartment. She got the towels and bounded back downstairs—and the woman was still standing like a plank next to the door. Those heels could not be comfortable, but she hadn't sat down.

What a weird woman.

She was squinting, annoyed, at her dead phone, but she looked up when Diana handed her the two towels.

"Thank you," she said.

"You're welcome to sit," Diana told her. She gestured to the chairs lining up a wall. "Don't worry about getting the chair wet or anything. I'm gonna make some coffee, do you want some?"

"Yes," the woman said.

All right. Diana went to make some coffee.

When she came back with a warm cup in each hand the woman was sitting in the chair farthest away from the desk. Her suitcase was beside her. She'd taken her coat off; under it, she was wearing a simple black pencil shirt and a formal white shirt, both soaked through. She was sitting on top of a towel so as to not get the chair wet. The other towel was around her shoulders, though she hadn't let down her hair.

She looked absolutely miserable.

It was so familiar. Where was Diana remembering her from?

She accepted the cup, barely lifting her eyes to thank Diana. Di lingered, eyes sweeping over the woman's features: her wide mouth, her pale skin, her dark, dark eyes, her thick brows. Her hands were bony, the fingers long. Her nails were perfectly manicured in a soft tan color, and Diana imagined them in a bright red instead—bright red and blue and purple and green and yellow, one color for each finger.

They'd spilled the yellow onto Diana's shirt and the entire afternoon had been spent trying to find a way to sneak back home and change her shirt without her mama seeing it.

"Cassandra," Diana said even before she'd realized the truth.

In front of her, with those dark eyes and that miserable set to her mouth, was her most precious childhood friend, Cassandra McNara.

"Excuse me?" she said, squinting up at Diana in suspicion. "How do you know my name?"

"Oh, man," Diana said. Her mouth broke open into a joyful grin. "It's *me*. Remember? *Diana?* Lady Di? We were neighbors, my mom was friends with your housekeeper, we played around the apartment complex, the other kids didn't really like us—remember when Peter dropped a whole jar of juice—"

"—on my new shirt," Cassandra whispered. "My parents were furious. You sneaked in after they scolded me and gave me Roberta to keep me company at night."

"And you never gave me my damn doll back."

"Lady Di," she said, and stood up at once. "Christ. Look at you. It's been—it's been *fourteen years*."

Di stepped forward and they crashed into a hug—Cassie had always been taller but now she was thin enough Diana's arms went all around her and then more. She hugged Diana carefully, as if wary of touching her too much, even when Di buried her face in her shoulder and squeezed.

Now she was all wet too. She laughed.

"Good Lord, Cassie, why are you out at night in the rain like this?" She took a step back and shook her head. Cassie's face was flushed, if still pained. "Come on in, let me give you some clothes. You're going to get sick like this."

"No, it's—fine," Cassie said, eyes veering away. "The rain will stop soon enough—"

"Cassie, you're no bother at all," Diana said. "God's truth. I just found you, come on, you can't get sick and die on me. I may not have these fancy clothes like you, but I have a sweater—hey, is orange still your favorite color? I have an orange sweater."

"Well," Cassie said, awkward. "It's not."

Diana paused, mouth closing shut. "Well," she tried again taking a step back and then another. "I'm all wet and full of oil and dirt and stuff, so I've to go up anyway. You don't have to come if you don't want to. …there's food upstairs too, though, if you haven't had dinner yet."

"I…"

Cassandra looked at Diana and seemed at a loss for what to do.

"It's really no bother," Diana reassured one last time.

"Okay," Cassie said, letting her hands go. "Yes. Thank you for the kindness."

Diana smiled at her.

✳✳✳

Di opened her freezer and found an old frozen pizza that should be enough for the two of them while Cassie went to the bathroom to get changed; her clothes would be too short for her, but anything would be better than being soaking wet. Di went to preheat the oven and wondered if Cassie would let down her hair.

"Hello," Di heard, and when she turned around Cassie was standing somewhat awkwardly at the door to the kitchen. Her hair was still in a tight bun. Di sent her a smile

"Hey! You look good. Regarding dinner, if you want it? I've a frozen pizza I can just pop in the oven. Should be done quickly."

"Christ, *yes*," Cassandra said, then flushed at her own vehemence. Diana laughed, and Cassandra lowered her gaze in embarrassment. "Ah—I haven't eaten pizza in... in *years*, honestly. You know how my parents are."

"You still live with them?" Diana asked as she popped the pizza into the oven. "You'd wanted to get out of their way as soon as possible."

Cassie looked away. "They're not home often," she said. "What about your parents? Your mom used to say she was going to keep her babies home until you were forty or more, yet here you are."

"Ah," Diana said. She rubbed the back of her head with a hand—it wasn't something she liked to talk about, but it'd been many years.. "Well. She totally would have. They, uh, died eight years ago. Car crash."

"Oh," Cassandra said, her voice small. She stared at Diana before veering her gaze away. "I...I'm sorry for your loss."

"I'm sorry for yours, too" Diana said. "Though... I *am* a bit glad you didn't suffer through the whole clusterfuck that it was."

"They're—they were *your* parents, Diana, not mine."

She flapped a hand. "Shut up, you know what I mean, they loved you. It's been eight years for me already, so it's... it's not that bad. I mean, I've been worse. But we're okay now. I got my own business!"

"You do?" Cassandra said, surprised. She finally approached Diana in the kitchen, standing a little ways from her. "You used to say you'd live off your folks' money and never work a day in your life."

"All the money was sucked up by hospital bills! So I had to become a hard worker, unfortunately.

Also, Cassie, you were just *in my business.* Downstairs? Did you think I was just an employee?"

"You're a mechanic?"

Diana lifted her eyebrows at her palpable surprise.

"Yes, yes, no one was more surprised. But I had a knack for it, and here we are." She leaned back against the counters and Cassie hesitantly stood beside her. When had Cassandra become such a skittish cat? "What're you doing right now?"

Cassie shrugged. "I'm just working at my parents' company. I'm an accountant."

"Ah." That... wasn't good news, Diana thought. It was the one thing Cassie had always said she wouldn't do. Diana kicked a leg forward, poking her calf. "There's still a lot of life to live, though. Who knows where you'll be tomorrow."

"Thank you for letting me in," Cassie said instead, cutting the conversation short. Diana couldn't fault her for not wanting to talk about it. "The wind was too harsh for my umbrella and none of my siblings could pick me up. You really saved me."

"Oh, yeah, how're they? Lord, I don't even remember the order of birth of you all. There's Michaela, Henry, Gabriel... Iris? Then Jamie—"

"Then me, then Isabella," Cassandra completed for her. They smiled at each other for a moment; listing all of the McNara kids had been an old joy of Diana's family. "Everyone's... the same."

"Ah, still assholes."

Cassandra laughed. Diana felt satisfied getting Cassie to laugh. Cassie rolled her eyes at her.

"Let's watch some TV," she said.

"Hell yeah," Lady Di agreed.

She got the pizza, plated some slices, and they moved to the living room. Diana was glad Cassie didn't comment on how small and messy the place was. The TV and the couch were old and even the curtains were dusty. Diana caught Cassie looking around, eyeing the mess with something like distaste.

Well, it was what Diana could afford, or at least what she was *willing* to afford.

Cassie sat down right next to Di so that they would touch from shoulders to knees and they ate in a somewhat comfortable silence. It was late and they were both tired.

"You could come by sometime," Di said during a commercial break. She licked pizza grease from her fingers and caught Cassandra staring.

Well, it wasn't like they'd remembered to bring napkins!

"Excuse me?"

"Pass by sometime," she repeated. "You know where I live now. I want to see you again. Let's eat pizza and watch stupid TV again."

Cassandra was silent for a moment.

"Do you still love cappuccinos, Diana?" she asked, turning to her with a serious look on her face. "There's a new café not far from here that I've been meaning to visit. It'd be my treat, of course, after your kindness today. You own your own business, you can give yourself a free afternoon sometime, right? We could meet up."

Diana put the slice of pizza down and pressed a hand to her heart.

"Cassie, you're offering to buy me coffee? You're an angel. You're an angel who came down to shine light into my life. Let's do it. I'm free whenever."

"I'm free… Thursday. Possibly Friday."

"Give me your phone number, then you can just call me later when you're sure when you'll be free."

"Yeah," Cassie said.

Di sent her a smile, and for once Cassie relaxed and gave her a nice grin back.

Chapter Two

Cassandra sat at her desk and stared at the clock at the bottom right of her computer's screen. Time had never passed slower. It was positively tortuous. She had work to do—not any that she cared about, but with only thirty minutes to go before midday struck and she could leave to see Di, there wasn't much else for her to distract herself with.

It was eleven thirty. Just thirty more minutes.

Wait, she did have a few emails to send. Maybe if she wrote really slowly…

There was a knock on the door of her tiny office. She looked up just in time to catch her oldest sister Michaela's expression of distaste before it was smoothed into something bland and polite.

She was shorter than Cassie, but had much more of a presence. She looked utterly like their father: she had his lighter brown hair and his piercing blue eyes, his strong jaw, and the disappointed tilt to his mouth. Cassandra was very familiar with that disappointed tilt, from basically everyone in her life.

"Hello," Cassandra said. "What can I help you with?"

"Margaret needs help writing the minutes of the last two meetings I've had," her sister said. She waved a hand. "You know how she is. I'd like it done for today, or at *best* tomorrow."

Ah, yes, Michaela's secretary Margaret. She often needed Cassandra's help for things she was paid to do, which Cassandra was *not* paid to do. But it wasn't any less boring or unfulfilling than the work she was actually paid to do, so why not?

This was how all Cassandra's siblings managed to get her help with everything.

However—

"I've only got thirty minutes until my lunch break," Cassandra said, "so please only send her by after I return."

There was a moment of palpably surprised silence.

"You have never been one to care much about things like lunch breaks," Michaela said.

"I'm hungry," Cassandra said with a shrug.

"...I see," her sister replied, because there wasn't much else she could say. "I will send Margaret over after you come back, then. And don't forget to answer the email our parents have sent you, Cassandra. They've told me you've yet to answer and it's been a week."

Ah, her parents' email. It was as bland and impersonal as an email could *be*, and it was laughable that they'd asked Michaela to nudge her into answering. They cared very little for Cassandra, as she cared very little for them.

"Yes," Cassandra said. "I will."

Michaela left. Cassie checked the hour again and thought that at least this useless conversation had eaten up a few minutes.

***

Cassandra actually left work five minutes after she'd intended to—but she didn't arrive late as she'd feared, and actually waited fifteen minutes in front of the café before Diana arrived. She checked her wrist watch several times. Her lunch break was an hour long and she didn't want to waste any precious time.

But her annoyance disappeared when Diana rounded the corner and grinned at the sight of Cassandra.

She was wearing roughly the same clothes as the last time they'd seen each other: loose trousers and a tight tank top that *really* put her cleavage into evidence, not that Cassandra occupied her eyes with such things, Diana was her *childhood friend*. Her dirty-blond hair was tied up in the tiniest pony-tail in the world.

Her face and her shirt and her arms were all streaked with grease and other dirty things, but she didn't seem at all bothered by them—or even aware of them, since she stepped up to wrap Cassie up in a tight hug without hesitating.

After a second, Cassie decided to just forget about the stains and hug her back. Damn, Diana's hugs were so good, she thought; she had such beautiful muscular arms.

"Hey," Diana said, stepping back. "Sorry for being a bit late! I've no excuse, I just got distracted."

"It's all right," Cassandra said, and though she'd been annoyed now it was true. "I haven't been waiting long. Shall we?"

"Hell yes. I'm going to order a cappuccino and the biggest piece of brownie humanly possible."

They walked in and quickly sat down at a small table by the window. The view wasn't the best—just the street—but it did give them a nice illusion of privacy. Cassie looked out and wished with all her heart that no one from her family nor anyone that knew her family would pass by and see her.

She turned back to Diana, who was inspecting a small pamphlet with coffee options, and smiled.

"So you still have the biggest sweet tooth in the world? Good to know."

"Christ, you haven't seen Manny," Di said, looking up at her. "The money I spent on dentists for that girl... I don't like to think about it. Oh, they have cappuccino with cinnamon. I'll get up and order, you keep our table. What'll you have?"

"Ah, just a small black coffee."

Diana lifted her eyebrows. "It's lunch time! You have to eat something."

Cassie shrugged. "Get whatever pastry you think is better." She reached for her bag and picked up her wallet. She gave Diana a fifty-dollar bill. "Here. It's my treat, remember? For your kindness."

"Oh, boy. *fifty dollars*, Cassie? What do you think we're buying, here?"

"It's for all the brownies you were eyeing on the menu."

"Caught me there. I'll be right back."

She got up and went to the counter. Cassie looked at her as she went and kept looking at her as they waited for her turn. Diana had grown so much in those fourteen years—and most of all she'd grown completely different than Cassie would have thought. At twelve years old, Diana had been a spoiled, beloved brat, but now she was confident and competent and responsible. She had her own business and she took care of her sister when their parents died.

Manuela had to have been young, then.

She wanted to *know* what had happened in Di's life in all those fourteen years when she'd been away which felt like a yawning chasm between who they'd been and who Cassandra wanted them to be *now.* She longed for the friendship they lost, the encouragement she didn't receive, the funeral she didn't get to go to. It hadn't been fine, but it'd been *bearable*, before: childhood friends lose contact all the time.

But they found each other again, and here they were now, drinking coffee like strangers. Cassandra found herself annoyed with the universe. If they'd find each other again, why had the gap been necessary? Why keep them from each other for *fourteen years?*

"You sure do look lost in thought."

Cassie startled. Diana laughed at whatever spooked expression she'd made, arms loaded with a tray full of...

"Christ, Lady Di, have you bought the entire store?"

She laughed again. She looked so *pleased*—with her face flushed and her green eyes bright, she looked positively joyful. She set the plate on top of the table and picked up her big cup of cappuccino.

"It's so cute how you still call me *Lady Di*," she said. "Even Jimmy doesn't call me that anymore!"

Cassandra focused in her own side of the tray, embarrassed. She picked up her own small black coffee and decided to ignore the five kinds of pastries Diana had bought.

"I can stop," she said. "I suppose it just comes out by itself—I didn't really mean to—"

"Hey, it wasn't a complaint," Di interrupted, easy and light. "It's no problem, Cassie. It's actually really cute."

Cute.

"I'm not cute," Cassandra said.

"Uh-huh," Diana agreed, a doubtful expression on her face. "But *is* everything all right? You were pretty spaced out there."

"Ah. It was nothing," Cassandra said. She picked out what appeared to be a harmless croissant. "I was thinking of these fourteen years, actually. It seems pointless that they've happened if we were just going to meet each other again."

"That's life," Diana said with a shrug. She took a bite of a piece of brownie. "Honestly, Cassie? I don't care. I'm just glad you're here now. Even if—I don't know, if we grew up too different, if we end up not becoming friends again or anything like that... I'm still glad I found you again."

"Oh," Cassandra said, stunned. She had definitely not thought of it like that. "I... me too."

Diana grinned at her.

"Hey, will you eat your croissant already? I'm already at my second brownie here!"

"Right, right," Cassie said.

"I can't believe my wisdom stunned you into silence."

"Apparently you have your moments."

"Every moment is my moment! I'm full of wisdom, Cassandra. Motherhood does that to a person."

"Motherhood?" Cassie asked, alarmed.

"I meant my baby sister!" Diana said with a laugh.

They spoke on. The subject changed every few moments: they spoke of the weather and of Diana's business and of Manuela's college, of Cassandra's long hair and the freckles she hid with make-up ("Seriously, *why*?" Diana asked. "They are *so beautiful*." Cassandra blushed a lot.) and her one younger sister Isabella. Cassandra disliked her home and Diana didn't really care about hers. Diana wanted to buy her own motorcycle and Cassandra seriously needed to start going to the gym.

Cassandra received many texts as one hour turned into two, then three. Michaela asked her where she was and her secretary Margaret sent her increasingly pleading messages. Her second oldest brother Gabriel asked about the emails he'd asked her to send. Her third oldest sister Jamie wanted help with something to do with finances. Isabella wanted to know where she was, and when she'd be home.

Above all of those sat the notification about the email her parents had sent, and as Diana and Cassandra finished their pastries and leaned more and more toward each other, all of them went, for once, blissfully unanswered.

***

They took their empty plates and mugs to the counter and left with arms linked. Cassandra looked down at short, short Diana and wanted to hold her under her arm, but didn't. They walked slowly toward Diana's shop, since it was very close, and Cassandra found herself relaxed like she'd never felt in her life.

Diana was so easy, so confident, so straight-forward. Being with her felt like heaven after spending so much time around her stupid stuck-up siblings.

It felt like a miracle, being with her again.

"Let's meet again," Cassandra said. "Sometime. I will most definitely not be able to free an entire afternoon again, but perhaps on the weekend?"

Di laughed. "It's Friday. Are you saying you want to meet again tomorrow?"

"Yes," Cassie said, then flushed. "If you're free? I have literally nothing to do."

"I really wanted to finish working on this car I'm working on right now," Diana said, scratching at her cheek. "Maybe next week? Or… I guess we don't need to have lunch again! What time does your shift end? We could have dinner!"

Cassandra recalled the last several years of her life where she arrived home at eleven at night.

"Six in the afternoon," she told Di. "I'd be very happy with dinner."

"I'm more of a home dinner, though. Instead of fancy restaurant dinner."

"I know a place," Cassandra told her, and found herself smiling. "I went there once and haven't found an excuse to pass by again. It's homey. I think you'd like it."

They arrived at the door of Diana's shop. Di unlinked their arms and stood by the door.

"I'd love it," she said, a sweet smile on her face.

Cassandra looked at that smile and felt her heart skip a beat.

Oh, no.

Chapter Three

Diana looked over old Jamie's bike and found it gleaming red and perfect. She passed the wet rag over it one last time and stood up from the stool, her back creaking up a storm when she straightened up.

She thought about work as she made her way to her apartment upstairs. She gobbled down some lunch.

She thought about work, and she thought about Cassandra.

They'd just been twelve when Cassandra and her enormous family moved away, but still at only twelve Cassie had been a rebel, in her quiet way—she had wanted to get away from her family, from her distant, cruel siblings and uncaring parents, she swore she wouldn't go into the family company, that she'd become an artist.

Of course, they'd just been kids and Cassandra had just doodled little kid things, but…

Cassandra now looked miserable—though she'd grown up beautiful, too. She was tall, her fingers long, her eyes very dark. Diana wanted—

Diana shook her head. She ate the last of Jimmy's lasagna and stood up.

… she worked and worked and thought of Cassandra all day long.

***

Diana took a shower and *severely* missed her childhood bathtub. Oh, what wouldn't she give to take a *bath*, to lay down in hot water with some bubbles and some wine… One day, when her sister finished college and had a job and was properly out there in *life*, Di was going to save some money and move somewhere with a big, nice bathroom.

She scrubbed the dirt out of her hair and stepped out, and decided to lay down on her couch instead. She wondered what Cassandra was doing then and there, then realized that she had her number after all.

Diana snapped a picture of her legs stretched out, with the TV visible over her feet with her bottle of wine between her thighs.

Diana: How's YOUR Saturday night going? :)

Cassie answered almost *instantly.*

Cassie: I'm just wrapping up some things at work. I should be going home soon, though.

Diana: …I'd say "it's already 10pm", but I also just finished up work too…

Cassie: I suppose we both stay at work until late.

Diana: I think if we went back in time and told our 10 year old selves we'd both be workaholics, we'd think we were mad.

Diana: I don't even have a bath): I'm having to drink my wine laying on the couch instead, like a peasant.

Cassie: I've a bathtub if you want to make use of it. I can't remember the last time I used it. Showers just seem more practical.

Diana: Cassandra, how DARE YOU. You HAVE a tub but you don't use it?

Diana: Give it to me): !

Diana: But for real, was that invitation a joke or not? Because if not, then I want to tell you that I'll be going to your apartment TOMORROW.

Diana: I've been dreaming of a bath for YEARS.

Cassie: No, it wasn't a joke.

Diana: Oh, man. SWEET.

Diana: What were you even doing at work so late? At least I just need to walk up the stairs to get home…

Cassie: Just some random things that needed to get done. There is always something that needs seeing to, apparently.

Diana: Yeah.

The conversation stagnated. Diana drank more wine and got distracted by the TV for a moment.

Cassie: I'd be glad to have you over.

Cassie: Perhaps after our dinner date?

Dinner date? Like a… *date?*

Diana shook her head. Of course Cassie didn't mean it like a *romantic date.* And Diana wasn't *interested* in her, anyway, even if she could help but notice how beautiful she'd grown. Diana had always envied her dark brown eyes, the sweet freckles around her face that seemed fainter than ever now.

They were just reconnecting, that was all.

Diana: That'd be awesome, yeah, since I wouldn't have to skip work twice.

Diana: We ended up not setting a date for that date, though, and now it's already Sunday…

Cassie: I'm sorry. I should have sent you a message like we'd agreed.

Cassie: I did not mean to ignore you, or to give the impression I didn't want to go, or anything of the sort. I'm sorry.

Diana drunk some more wine and felt surprised. For a moment she thought about calling Cassandra. Suddenly it wasn't enough to be talking to her through text; she wanted to hear her voice, see her face.

Maybe Di was just a bit more tipsy than she'd meant to be.

Diana: Hey, it's fine. It's nothing, Cassie. I know you're a busy woman and all, and besides I had your number too. I could have called.

Diana: Hey, remember when we were ten and you got your first cellphone? I pestered my parents for MONTHS to get me one too, just so we could call each other from across the damn room.

Cassie: Good Lord, I remember. I think I still have that phone thrown around here somewhere.

Diana: Oh my God, just throw it away. Also, must tell me when you're free and we can meet!

Diana: I really want to see you.

Diana: It feels like nothing's been right ever since you left, which is a bit pathetic, since we were TWELVE.

Diana nearly dropped her phone when it started ringing. She stared at it, dumbfounded. It was Cassie, because of course it was. It was almost as if she'd known Diana had wanted to call her.

It almost felt like when they were children, when they didn't ever need words to know how the other was feeling, was thinking. They'd been closer than sisters. Losing her had been like losing a limb.

"Hey," Diana said, bringing the phone to her ear.

"Hello," Cassandra said very seriously.

Diana laughed.

"Hey, Cassie. What're you calling me for?"

"I'm sorry," Cassie said, voice low. "I wouldn't have left if I'd had a choice, I didn't know they were going to cut contact between us. It's been hard, too, without you. I'm sorry I could not send letters like I'd promised. They didn't let me. I didn't mean to leave you."

"It's not your fault," Diana said, shaking her head even though Cassie couldn't see it. She curled her legs to her chest. "I knew something must have happened. I know how your parents are."

"They have not changed one bit," Cassie said dryly.

"It seemed silly," Diana told her, closing her eyes against the confession. This wasn't something she'd told anyone—but this was Cassie and Diana was loose and full of wine, and was not someone prone to shyness besides. "To miss you so much, I mean. The more I grew, the more it was… you were just my tiny childhood friend. It wasn't like we'd actually meant any of our silly promises. It wasn't like it was going to last. It's rare that people keep in touch. Right? But I still—"

"I know," Cassie said. "Me too."

They were in silence for a moment.

"I—I can make time tomorrow," Cassandra said. "I've never taken a day off, no one will have moral standing to scold me if I leave for lunch and don't return."

Di pressed her face against her couch and grinned.

"We can lunch, then?" she asked.

"Yes," Cassie said. "I can come by your place. I know a restaurant not far away."

"...then the bath?"

"Then the bath," Cassandra said, and Diana heard her smile through the phone.

***

Diana sat on a bench she dragged up to her kitchen and watched Jimmy as he washed her dishes. She had her cheek propped up on a hand while the other twirled her phone around. She'd been talking to Cassie—as she often was, these days—but she went off to do something for work and hadn't come back.

As for Diana, it was Tuesday but a Jimmy-imposed workless day.

"Di, if you don't put that phone somewhere else, it'll end up soaked in water," Jimmy said dryly.

"I'm not the one washing the dishes," she said with a roll of her eyes. "Which, again, you don't *have* to do, Jimmy. I don't *actually* invite you over to clean my house and cook me food, you know that, right?"

"If I don't do it, this place becomes a mess and you end up eating garbage!"

"I don't eat *only* garbage!"

"Yeah, you eat garbage *and* what I cook for you."

"Whatever," Diana said. "I thought you wouldn't be able to come for a couple of *weeks*, old man. What gives?"

"What gives is that I do what I want, Diana."

"Uh-huh," Di said, unconvinced. "I knew the reasons you gave for your absence were flimsy, but I didn't think they were flimsy enough you managed to come by anyway."

"My children know nothing," he muttered. "They're all like *Dad, you're not going to that girl's house again, are you? Has she started paying you yet?* I'm tired of it! If they listened to me, this wouldn't happen."

"Well, it's not really their fault," Diana said, looking down. "They worry about you, that's all. God knows I'd worry about Manny if she went off to play housekeeper to some random person."

Jimmy shut off the water.

"You're not a random person," he said firmly. "And, Diana, repeat with me: I do what I want."

Di snorted.

"I do what I want, Diana, and what I want to do is make some chocolate mousse."

"Uh-huh. Right," she said. "You're not eating any of it though, right? Remember? Because of your diabetes?"

He muttered curses under his breath.

"Yeah, old man," she said, unamused. "I didn't forget the diabetes."

"Leave the kitchen," he said, waving a hand at her. Droplets of water and foam splashed on her face. "Go to the living room or something."

"And leave you here alone? You realize you've forbidden me from going to the garage, if you boot me from the kitchen then what am I going to do?"

"You make me weep when you say this kind of thing," Jimmy said, shaking his head. "Don't you have hobbies?"

"No."

"Don't you have that girlfriend?"

Diana felt her face flush.

"She's not my *girlfriend*, Jimmy, she's a childhood friend and that's all."

Jimmy sent her an unconvinced look. He looked pointedly at the cellphone she was clutching in her hands and then back up at her, point made without a single word.

"Normal friends can eagerly await their friend's messages," Diana said.

"Uh-huh," Jimmy said. "Right. When she answers, do say hi. I'd like to meet this nice Cassie of yours. Maybe she'll help you with that awful lack of hobbies thing."

Chapter Four

Cassandra arrived at work about two hours late and felt the entire world staring at her the entire way there, as if everyone knew what a disgrace she was. A part of her knew it wasn't so bad—she could count the number of times she'd arrived late in the fingers of *one hand*—but she still felt bad.

She'd just stayed up too late talking to Diana. She was allowed to do that at least once.

She sat down at her desk in her cramped office and felt a headache forming in the back of her skull. She wanted more than anything to let her hair loose, but she hated it, and so it stayed in its tight bun. One day she'd cut it all off; and this was something she'd been promising herself for decades.

As she'd expected, it didn't take long for Michaela to knock on her door and let herself in.

She looked as tall and stiff as always, though today the disappointed tilt to her mouth was even more pronounced.

"Hello," Cassandra said. "What can I help you with, Michaela?"

"I couldn't help but notice," she said, "you didn't return to work yesterday after your lunch hour. So, perhaps you shouldn't think about what you can help me with right now, but what you said you would help my *secretary* with *yesterday*."

"Ah, of course. You can let her in whenever is best for you."

Michaela relaxed a bit at Cassandra's easy acceptance as if she'd been afraid her one moment of rebellion had meant she'd become another person. She looked at Cassie almost curiously.

"What were you doing out there?"

"Lunch took longer than expected," Cassie said, which was the actual truth, if not the complete one. "I thought it would be fine, since I often stay longer than when my shift ends."

Michaela regarded that with indifference.

"Do not do it again," she said, and left without another word.

Ah, family, Cassandra thought, and already missed Diana.

***

Cassandra helped Margaret and wondered not for the first time why on *earth* Michaela hadn't fired the woman yet.

Not that it mattered, at least to Cassandra. But wondering about it was certainly a way to pass the hours, her work being so boring that she only needed half her brain for it. She only managed to stay in her office for another half an hour after Margaret left before her least oldest sister Jamie walked in and sat sprawled over the armchair in the corner of the office.

"Hey, little sis," she said, far too cheerful, and then roped Cassandra into helping her with her personal finances for nearly two hours.

Cassandra contemplated locking her office door after Jamie left and thought about Isabella. Her younger sister worked here at the company too, and was surely somewhere doing anything but working.

Cassie picked up her phone. There were no unread messages.

Cassandra: Hello, Isabella.

Cassandra: Would you like to have lunch together today?

Isabella: Only if it's at the sushi place.

Cassandra sighed. The sushi place Isabella liked wasn't a cheap place. But Cassie remembered Diana's tiny apartment, and her little comments, and thought about how much money of hers sat unused. Why should she worry so much about a restaurant being expensive if she didn't have to worry about money?

She could do this, for her little sister.

Maybe she could take Diana to this restaurant one day. Cassandra wondered if she liked sushi. She seemed more like a chicken wings kind of person, but then Cassie was pretty sure that pasta she'd eaten at her place had been homemade...

She shook her head. She shouldn't be thinking so much of Diana.

Cassandra: Yes, the sushi place is fine.

Isabella: Oh man! We haven't been there in ages!

***

Her workday went on without any issues other than Michaela's displeasure and a few whispering people, which didn't stop her from leaving the *second* 5:59 p.m. turned into 6 p.m. How many extra hours had she poured into this company just for the sake of having something to do?

She had someone to meet, now, and was not keen on staying here one second more than strictly needed.

***

Cassie arrived quickly at Diana's place—it still both surprised her and saddened her that Diana had been so close all this time, perhaps for years, without them finding each other. The reception area was empty except for a bored looking boy behind the desk, staring at his phone.

She approached him and he blinked when he caught sight of her.

"Oh, are you Cassandra?" he asked. "Diana's in the garage, waiting for you."

Cassie nodded and went. The garage smelled of cars, oil, and heat. The walls were dark and filled with bulletin boards and posters, which made the space seem smaller than it truly was. Diana was hunched over a desk shoved into the corner of the room, one leg raised to her chest on the small stool and her thumb on her mouth—she was biting her nail in concentration, eyebrows furrowed.

She was wearing loose trousers and a tight tank-top as she often did; Cassandra flushed and looked away, because looking at Diana's cleavage was rude no matter how big it was. Her dark blond hair was loose around her face; it went down to her chin and was just a bit wavy. Cassandra wanted, for a hot moment, to card her fingers through it.

She was beautiful.

"Hello," Cassandra said, voice rough.

Diana looked up at her with her emerald eyes shining. Her smile lit up her entire face.

"Cassie!"

She stood up at once and squeezed Cassie into a tight hug. Wow, she was small but so *strong*. Her arms must be twice the size of Cassie's. Cassandra tried not to think about it, least she start blushing wildly in her childhood friend's presence.

"Man, you're early!" Lady Di said and finally let go of her. Her smile lingered in the corner of her lips. Cassandra found herself smiling back. "I was planning on going up to take a shower before you showed up."

"I'm not really," Cassie told her. "I'm just in time."

"Oh," Diana said, scratching her cheek. "Seriously? It's already past six? I lost track of time, it seems. Would you mind waiting?"

Cassie cocked her head to the side. "For your shower? I thought you were going to take a bath after dinner. You seemed so excited about my bathtub."

Diana's joy grew tenfold.

"If you're still letting me, I'm still going, but I'd have to take a shower before a soak anyway," she said. "And anyway, I wouldn't want us to go have dinner with grease in my hair."

"There's no grease in your hair," Cassandra reassured her.

"Oh, you flatter me."

"I don't mind waiting," Cassandra said. "Take as long as you want."

So they went; Diana left Cassandra in her small living room and left to take her shower. Cassandra stood awkwardly and looked around before she realized Di was away and there was no reason to feel awkward. She walked softly around and peered at things. She wasn't nosy, really, she just—she had no excuse. She was feeling nosy. She wanted to *know* what had happened in Di's life during all the years they'd been apart.

She peered at the photographs around the small TV. Most of them were of Manuela. Cassie let her eyes linger on one of Harriet and Roberto, Diana's parents.

Cassie would never see them again.

Diana took less time in her shower than Cassandra thought humanly possible. In no time at all there she was walking into the living room. She wore, for the first time Cassie had seen, skinny jeans with her usual tank-top.

Cassandra looked away, a very red blush rising on her face, and tried not to look too much at her *childhood friend's* legs. Di gently toweled her hair before she threw the towel at the couch and turned to Cassie.

"Let's go!" she said.

***

Cassie had been right when she thought that this was the kind of place Diana would love; it was a small thing Cassie had found a long time ago and never managed to make time to visit again. It was homey and low-priced, the kind of place her siblings would never go to—and of course it wasn't fun to go out by herself. She could of course come with Isabella, but...

Isabella, too, had better things to do than to go out with Cassandra all the time.

Di seemed positively *charmed*, though, as they walked in and sat down on a table near a window. She peered at the paintings hung around and admired the menu's offerings. She commented on the beautiful view outside and sat very, very close to Cassie on the cushioned wall-seats.

Cassie really did not mind.

"Oh, risotto," Diana said appreciatively.

"Get whatever you want," Cassandra told her, not really paying attention to the menu Di was holding up for the two of them. Di had a mole right beside her right eye and it was lovely. "I'll pay, of course."

"Ah, Cassie—"

"I'm repaying your kindness," Cassie told her.

Diana eyed her. "You already did that, remember?"

"Do you think your kindness was worth just a cup of coffee?"

"And that *entire tray of food*. Come on, Cassie," Diana denied, shaking her head. She set the menu down. "I'll pay this time. There's no reason for you to spend more money."

"You know I have money," Cassandra told her honestly. "I'd be happy to spend it with you."

"Okay." Di nodded. "Then you can pay on our next dinner date."

Cassandra felt her face heat up at the idea of another dinner *date*.

"And anyway, I want to treat you too!" Diana exclaimed. "So get whatever you want, and it's my treat this time."

"Sure," Cassie said faintly. "Whatever you want."

When they walked out of the restaurant, Diana held her hand. It was very warm compared to

Cassie's, not bony or sweaty. They had held hands as kids, so this didn't mean anything else—just a reconnection, a familiarity, a way to take back something they'd lost.

Still, Cassandra's heart raced.

Cassandra's place was a good walk away, but Diana didn't seem to mind. The way wasn't exactly beautiful, but Diana spoke of the blooming trees and pet the stray cats she could and Cassandra found herself appreciating those things as well.

"I never go out much," Diana said. "'cept to the store, to get groceries, or to buy more things for the shop. It's nice to just walk like this and pet the cats, you know?"

"Yeah," Cassandra said, which was a bland, but truthful answer. "I never go out either."

"Too busy working?" Di asked dryly.

"You're a workaholic too," Cassie said with a frown.

"...yeah, but I love what I do," Di said. "I don't mean to judge or anything, but you pretty clearly don't like where you are. I just can't help remember all the things you said when we were kids. For you this really would have been the worst case scenario."

"Yeah," Cassie said. "I—I don't know. It just sort of happened."

"Do you still draw?"

"No," Cassie said. "I stopped a long time ago."

"Oh."

"It just sort of happened," Cassie repeated, looking own. "Even when I wanted to be an artist I knew going to college for it wouldn't amount to much, so why not do accounting like they wanted? They were paying anyway. Why search for a job elsewhere when I had a guaranteed one in the family company? Why go out there and pay rent when I can live in our building?"

"I know," Lady Di said. "God knows I would have done *anything* to have that kind of security, these last eight years."

"Security," Cassandra repeated—and it didn't feel like the right word.

It was all too *stifling* to call it *security*. Too unfulfilling. It left her too empty. And yet it really was the right word, wasn't it? Cassandra was stuck inside the safe bubble of her family's money, and that meant she didn't have freedom or *happiness*, but still she didn't pay rent and she'd never go hungry.

It'd been enough, all these years.

"It's all fine, though," Cassandra told her. "I'm fine."

"You could still draw, though," Di told her, choosing not to comment on Cassie's obvious lie. "It's not like you don't have time. Goodness, Cassie, we're twenty six, not *sixty*. And even at sixty there'd still be time. I bet you have enough money saved by now you could move out without trouble."

Cassandra thought about her boisterous funds, largely untouched.

"Well," she said. "Yes."

"It's something to think about," Di said. "Who's stopping you from just doing whatever the hell you want?"

Cassie opened her mouth to answer: so many people, Michaela and her other siblings, her parents, her *life*, everything—but her mouth clicked shut and she said nothing instead. Because—as always—Diana was in her simple way *right*.

Who was stopping her?

"Who knew you'd grow wise, Diana," Cassie said instead.

"Hey!"

***

Diana *ooh*'d and *aah*'d at everything in Cassandra's apartment.

"It's so big!" she said, and: "Look at this veranda! This *view!*" and: "This is the biggest kitchen I've ever seen!" and: "Oh my God, I've never sat on such a comfortable couch."

"It came with the apartment," Cassandra said awkwardly.

She didn't exactly like her apartment. It was in her parents' names, and thus she couldn't really redecorate like she wanted to, and many of the things inside it had come with the place. Still, having Diana swooning over everything made her flush in pleasure.

Hopefully Diana wouldn't notice, like she seemed to not have noticed the many times Cassandra blushed in her presence.

The grand tour ended, of course, at Cassandra's bathroom. Diana gripped the door tightly and seemed too overcome with feelings to speak. Even if Cassandra didn't much care for it she had to admit it was very beautiful: it was all white tiles and fluffy white towels and soft flowers around..

The bathtub was huge.

"I just noticed I forgot to bring clothes and a towel," Diana said faintly.

"You can have some of mine," Cassandra reassured, and tried not to picture Diana in her clothes.

"Christ, Cassandra. You're telling me you have *this* in your bathroom and you choose to take *showers*?"

"It's unpractical and wasteful to fill this stupid thing every time I come home from work."

"Doesn't have to be every time! You could do it, like, twice a month. I'm going to be here so often, just a warning."

"You can come here anytime you want," Cassandra said, too honestly.

Chapter Five

That bathroom was the most beautiful thing Diana had ever seen and she loved it—though she thought it didn't fit Cassandra at all. The practical woman who wore those bland coats and spoke stiffly even when being casual didn't seem like the type of person who'd appreciate this kind of open, flowery space.

Case in point: she only took showers even when she had *this bathtub*.

Diana loved it enough for both of them.

The tub took a long time to fill. Diana peered at the bottles around it and chose one to dump into the tub; she'd have a bubble bath no matter what. She didn't feel shy about taking Cassandra's stuff, since most of it was *still sealed.* Christ. Diana needed to get Cassie into this tub.

It wasn't big enough for two people, was it? They could try, though. It wouldn't be weird to take a bath together, right? The thought of it made Diana's heart beat faster, even when she knew she shouldn't think those things—the thought of Cassie naked. Her skin was so pale, it'd probably turn all pink from the heat. Maybe she'd let her hair down from that tight bun. Maybe she'd relax a bit. It wasn't weird to think of these things, right?

They'd just reconnected. The last thing they needed was for Diana to go ahead and start thinking of her friend naked.

Even if she was so very beautiful.

Well, it wasn't like Cassie would ever *know*, Diana reasoned with herself, a hand submerged in the tub. There was no thought police! Diana could think of whatever she wanted!

God, she wanted some wine.

She chucked her clothes off and got herself into the tub. The hot water dissolved all her problems away. Lack of money? Slow business? Weird, creepy clients? None of them mattered. Diana relaxed so thoroughly she felt like she'd never grow tense again. The bubbles were as tall as her. Everything was beautiful.

…she really wanted some wine.

Actually, she really wanted Cassandra. This had been about meeting again, being together, and God knew what Cassandra was doing out there alone. She got an arm out of the water, dried it haphazardly on a stray towel, and picked up her phone.

Diana: Cassie?

Diana: What're you doing out there?

Cassie: Nothing.

Diana: Nothing? Then you won't mind coming in here?

Diana: It doesn't feel right to be here but not with you. Is it weird to ask for you to come into the bathroom when I'm taking a bath?

Diana: I'm not shy about it if you're not.

Cassie took some time to answer. Diana closed her eyes and relaxed into her bath and wasn't nervous about it. *Cassandra* was probably fretting about being asked something like this, being who she was, but if it was too awkward for her, then it was all fine by Diana!

She really hoped Cassie would say yes, though.

Cassie: If it's okay with you?

Diana grinned.

Diana: It's not like the bubbles will let you see anything ;)

Cassie: I wouldn't want to infringe on your privacy.

Diana: Well, I'm the one who's inviting you, so...

There was a knock on the door.

"Come on in!"

Cassie walked in, stiff and awkward and with her eyes veering wildly around the room, anywhere but Diana. Di had to smile, though she stopped herself from laughing. It wasn't Cassie's fault she was embarrassed. She was blushing to the roots of her hair and down to her neck. Her pale face was blotchy from it.

She was beautiful.

"Don't be shy," Diana said, and Cassandra rolled her eyes.

"This is very unusual," she answered.

She sat down on the toilet, a bit away from the tub, and held her hands together on her lap like a proper lady. She sat completely straight, too, her back like a ruler and her feet together. It looked... uncomfortable. Diana remembered Cassie at ten, or eleven: her hair had been huge and always in braids, and she sat primly, too, but never so stiffly.

"You look so tense," Diana said, voice low. "Maybe you should get in here with me to loosen up some."

Cassie's face grew *even redder*. She looked at Di with wide eyes and spluttered.

"I—I—"

Diana laughed. Cassie deflated a little and lifted a hand to her own face, as if to try and cover up her enormous blush.

"Don't tease," she scolded.

"I'm not! I was being genuine! You're so *stiff* all the time, Cassie. Maybe it's because you haven't been using your bath at all."

Cassie looked away—eyes to the floor, to the ceiling. "Diana, I can—will you please lower yourself in the tub, your breasts are—ah—"

Diana lowered herself in the tub with another laugh.

"It's not like you haven't seen this before," she reasoned.

"When we were ten," Cassie retorted, glancing back at her. "They were significantly smaller."

"You can go if you want to," Di said. She crossed her arms on the rim of the tub and rested her chin there. "I don't want to make you uncomfortable. I just thought that being here, but not with you, was kind of against the point of being here, you know?"

"I don't want to go," Cassie told her. She finally relaxed some, leaning back with her ankles crossed. "It's fine, I'm just… not used to this. I don't know anyone as… extroverted as you. I apologize for—all this. My blushing."

"It's cute," Diana said.

Cassie flushed further. "Don't tease," she repeated.

"I'm not," Diana reassured. "You're cute, Cassie. You're very beautiful."

They looked at each other. Cassie opened her mouth and then closed it, unsure; Diana thought that she mustn't often hear this kind of thing and vowed to tell her friend she was beautiful as often as she could.

"...you too," Cassie said, awkward.

"Thanks," she said with a grin, and then remembered her cravings and perked up. "Hey, Cassie, since you're here—is it too rude to ask for some wine? Come on, it's like a childhood *dream* to drink wine in a big bathtub filled with bubbles!"

Cassie laughed, amused.

***

They quickly polished off the bottle of wine. Diana's fingertips grew wrinkly from staying so much in the water and Cassie eventually loosened up enough to sit cross-legged on the floor by the tub, closer to Diana. They spoke of their days, of random things, of TV shows and recipes and places to visit, but not of their families, or anything serious. Diana didn't want to think of the time they'd lost—only that they were here right now.

Eventually Di shooed Cassie off so she could dry. She dressed in the clothes Cassie had left for her: pajama pants and a nondescript cream-colored sweater. They smelled like a faint perfume and the sleeves went past Diana's fingers.

She decided then and there she was going to keep it.

When she left the bathroom she saw Cassie had changed, too, had put on loose trousers and the very sweater she'd taken from Diana that day they first saw each other.

Diana threw herself on the couch and ended up mostly on top of Cassie, but Cassie didn't seem to mind.

"What do you want to do?" Cassie asked. She arranged their limbs so that Diana had her legs over Cassie's lap and had a cheek on Cassie's shoulder but wasn't actively elbowing her on the stomach anymore. "If you're going to stay for longer. I know it's already a bit late."

"I don't even know what time it is," Diana told her.

Cassie checked her phone and lines appeared between her brows. "We should lock the door. I've been ignoring everyone and that includes Isabella, so the probability of her storming in here is basically one hundred percent."

"Your baby sis?"

"The youngest of us, yes. None of the others care."

That was one sad fucking phrase, but it wasn't like Di didn't remember from their childhood—Cassandra was the second youngest of *seven kids*, with an enormous age gap between she and Isabella and the other five. Those five really hadn't cared about her. It wasn't a surprise they still didn't.

"What're the others calling you for, then?" Di asked.

"Work stuff," Cassie said, resigned.

"Never mind that," Di said. "Let's watch a movie! Your TV is *huge*, man."

Cassie looked at her for a moment.

"Okay," she said, and turned off her phone for good.

***

They watched a random cooking show, this one about cakes, and grew steadily drowsier. Diana felt content to a degree she couldn't remember ever feeling before. She sat inside the bubble of Cassandra's increasingly bold arms and felt content.

Isabella burst into the room like Cassandra had expected. Cassie was too used to her to be phased by her dramatic entrance and Diana was too lazy in wine and warmth and good television to be bothered. If they were burglars or something, at least she'd die happy.

Instead, Isabella opened her mouth to shout and instead stared at the sight of her sister with a strange woman draped all across her on the couch.

Diana grinned up at her. "Hey, Bella!"

"What the fuck," Isabella said, baffled.

"This is Diana," Cassandra said without looking away from the TV. "I've spoken about her."

"Wow, how you've grown, Bella!" Diana exclaimed. "You're older than Manny, right? Man, you're so big. How old are you?"

"You're drunk," Isabella said.

"Tipsy," Diana corrected. "You must be… twenty-two."

"She is," Cassandra said, impressed.

"*You* weren't answering your *phone!*" Isabella shouted, pointing one accusing finger at Cassandra.

50

"I was otherwise occupied."

Diana pointed at herself with her thumb. Isabella recoiled.

"You didn't tell me the two of you were… like that.."

Cassie recoiled as if stung.

"Like what?" Diana asked.

"Diana is a childhood friend and we spent the afternoon together, as childhood friends," Cassandra said blandly, eyes still glued to the television. "Nothing more. If you're done judging me and shouting at me, Isabella, you're welcome to leave."

Nothing more, Diana repeated to herself. Isabella had assumed they were more than friends. As in, that they were *together.* Diana felt something flare up in her chest: something like satisfaction, like a surprised smugness, at the thought that Isabella would have thought that because Cassie had to like women like Diana and because they seemed close.

The thought rattled around in Diana's mind: Isabella had thought they were *together.*

"You know I didn't mean it *like that*," Isabella said, at once deflating.

Cassie stared straight at her sister. "What did you mean it like, then?" she asked.

"Cass," Isabella said, frustrated, "just answer your phone. That's all I ask. I literally just asked you this last week."

"I don't know what you fear will happen to me," Cassandra said. She tightened her hold around Diana almost defiantly. "We've been watching TV and

51

drinking wine. Don't fret. And go home, Isabella. I'm growing quite tired of your storming around here."

"I didn't know you were a mean drunk," Isabella said dryly. "I'll leave you here with your girlfriend, don't mind me."

"She's *not my girlfriend*, Isabella."

Isabella left the room without another word. Diana twisted her body so she could look up at Cassie, who was steadfastly looking at the TV. Her face was flushed; she seemed embarrassed and maybe a little afraid.

"Are you a lesbian?" Diana asked.

Cassie flinched with her whole body. She didn't say anything, eyes flitting back at Diana in fear. Diana struggle to sit up and cursed all the wine currently in her bloodstream. Cassie let her go easily, body lax, and didn't really look at Di as Di righted herself on the couch to sit properly.

"You don't have to tell me if you don't want to," Di said, even though Cassie's silence had been pretty telling in and of itself. "I guess I just want to make sure I understood what Isabella had meant with what she'd said. I'm not—I don't judge. I mean, it'd be pretty stupid and hypocritical of me to judge."

Cassie sent her a frown, head cocked to the side.

"Because, you know," Diana added. "*I* am a lesbian."

"Oh," Cassie said.

Diana watched her slowly relax, the hands that had been gripping tightly at the hem of her shirt slowly uncurl.

"I..." Cassie tried. "I don't know. I did... see girls. Once upon a time. I thought I was bi—but I just stopped."

"Why?" Diana said, trying to sound as gentle as she could. She didn't want to sound nosy, but she was *curious*. "Because you wanted to, or because of the things your family said? My own parents weren't that okay with it," Diana continued when Cassie just stayed silent. "They were starting to come around when they, well, died. I think they'd have been okay with it, given some time."

"I see," Cassie said.

"It's okay if you don't want to talk about it," Diana repeated.

"No, it's... it's fine," Cassie said, eyes bright. "I don't really talk about it."

"You can talk about it with me," Diana promised.

"Okay," Cassie whispered.

Chapter Six

Cassandra woke up in the morning with a small headache that would still surely ruin her day and stared at the ceiling. Morning sun was streaming in through her windows, and hitting her directly in the face. She didn't move away from it even though it made her headache worse.

Diana was gay.

Cassandra wanted to cover her face with her hands and scream. For some ungodly reason, the thought bounced around her head unwilling to be ignored, even though it shouldn't be such a huge thing, even though it shouldn't mean anything, change anything—of course it was funny that both of them ended up like this, but still Cassandra shouldn't think about it so much—

That Diana was gay, that was.

She thought about kissing Diana.

Oh, Christ, she thought, and covered her face with her hands.

When her phone buzzed on her nightstand, she was more than glad for the distraction. The last thing she needed was to linger on her stupid thoughts. And anyway just because she'd *thought* something didn't mean she actually *wanted* it or anything, no matter how beautiful, blond, single, green-eyed, muscular, and gay Diana was.

Cassandra picked up her phone with something like desperation.

"Hello, this is Cassandra McNara."

"Hey, Cass," Iris said. "I know it's *so very early* but can you meet me here at my place in, say, half an hour?"

Cassandra took her phone from her ear so she could stare at it. Iris was her second oldest sister and she lived on the other side of the town. And it was… Cassie checked her phone… five a.m.

"I cannot physically be at your apartment in half an hour," Cassie told her. "Henry lives closer to you. Perhaps he could help you?"

"You know how Henry is!"

Yes. Henry, unlike Cassandra, was not a huge pushover. Michaela, Henry, Gabriel, Iris, Jamie, or Isabella were neither of them pushovers.

"What do you need help with?" Cassandra asked, resigned, and sat up in bed.

***

She actually managed to get to work in time; she walked in at precisely eight in the morning, well-put together but feeling exhausted. Her hair was pulled tight in its bun, like always, and it was making her headache even *worse*. She thought again about just cutting it all *off*—and then remembered Diana's words.

Who's stopping you?

Cassandra shook her head. She didn't want to think about this. She made her way to her office and set her purse down. Her computer was slow to turn on. She fished her phone out of her bag. Maybe she should send Diana a message—

Oh, Michaela had sent her some texts the day before.

Michaela: Cassandra, come by my office.

Michaela: I've just been informed you've left already. You've never been so lax when it comes to your working hours. We'll need to speak about this later.

Since she was alone, Cassandra didn't resist the urge to roll her eyes. For years now she'd done nothing but work in this place and now she left after lunch *once* and left at *her actual end of shift* once and she'd "never been so lax" and they "needed to speak about it"?

She looked down at Michaela's messages from today.

Michaela: Assuming you've arrived on time and not late, again, I'm here to remind you to come by my office before lunch time. We will have that conversation and I still need you for what I had called you about yesterday, before I saw you had left with no warning.

Cassandra: Okay, she sent, and left it at that.

"Wow, I never saw you making this kind of face," came a light voice from the doorway of her office. "You look like how *I* look whenever our siblings try and talk to me."

Cassandra looked up. It was Isabella, who was leaning against the door with her arms crossed. Cassie couldn't remember the last time she'd been here, even if she worked at the company as well. Isabella was more of a free spirit; Michaela hadn't fired her yet probably just out of familial obligation.

"Hello," Cassie said, voice bland. She wasn't feeling very charitable after what had happened the day before.

Isabella straightened up, uncrossing her arms.

"Hi, Cass," she said. "You look mad at me."

"I am generally mad at those who out me like you did," Cassie agreed.

Isabella winced, which made Cassandra loosen up a bit. At least she felt bad about it.

"I *am* sorry about that, Cass," she said. "I was just surprised! I hadn't expected you to be like *that* with your weird childhood friend."

"She's not weird," Cassie protested. "And we're *not* like *that*, as you put it."

Isabella gave her an incredulous look.

"Were you not there, yesterday?" she asked, giving Cassie a *look.* "She was draped all over you like a possessive cat and you were *letting her*, and I'm pretty sure that sweater she was wearing was *yours—*"

"She took a bath, that's all!"

Isabella raised her eyebrows.

"She doesn't have a bathtub, so I let her use mine," Cassandra defended herself. "And besides, this isn't about me and Diana—but about what *you* did."

"I've apologized," Bella said dryly. "And anyway even if you and your Diana aren't *like that*, you still *want* to be with her."

Cassandra opened her mouth to tell her no and couldn't quite bring herself to lie.

"Aha! So you *do* like her!"

"I—" Cassandra tried, and felt a blush rise on her face. "I don't want to talk about this."

"Oh, we are going to talk about it. A lot. During lunch, at the sushi place, and you're going to pay even though I was an ass yesterday because I'm your baby sister and you love me."

Cassandra sighed.

***

Cassandra arrived home after a long day of work feeling tired and weary, as always, even if her lunch with Isabella had sweetened her day. She dragged herself to the living room. It was something like eleven p.m. and she was hungry, but she knew she didn't really have anything filling in her kitchen. She was so tired of eating veggie omelets.

She sat down on her couch. Just for a moment, she thought, and then she'd take a shower, eat whatever her kitchen could offer, and go to *sleep.*

She really wanted to eat something filling. Some bread. She didn't have bread and hadn't had it for some time.

Diana probably had bread at her house, Cassie thought idly.

Diana, who was gay.

Cassandra sighed at herself and at her stupid brain which wouldn't stop thinking these stupid things—especially after her conversation with Isabella. Cassandra didn't really want to admit it to herself, but her sister was devious and had forced it out of her: she liked Diana.

Diana, who was gay, and who, Cassie's brain added, could like Cassandra back.

She stood up from her couch and grabbed her phone from her bag on her way to her room, shedding clothes as she went. She dropped them all on top of her bed and considered for one wild moment just going to sleep right then and there, naked and without a shower. But she couldn't bear to.

She reached up to let her hair down—and noticed a light blinking on her phone, indicating a notification she hadn't seen. It was a message from Diana. Her mouth curled into a smile. She knew they both had work, but it was a sad day when Diana didn't send her anything on her phone.

It was a picture. Diana was standing in front of a mirror and making a pose that highlighted her curves. She was wearing a black tank top that showed off her stupid muscular beautiful arms and showed off her impressive cleavage. She was wearing tight dark trousers, unlike every single other time Cassie had seen her, and she had thighs to die for. She had streaks of grease in her hair, though not in her face, and was giving the camera a happy grin.

Cassandra felt something squeeze her lungs.

Christ, she thought, looking at that picture. Her eyes lingered on all the right places—Diana's face, her lips, her arms, her breasts, her hips, Christ, Cassandra thought, *Christ*, she was going to keel over dead.

Diana: Bought new jeans!

Diana: They look brand new, don't they? But I got them at a thrift store. What a STEAL.

Cassandra wondered what the fuck she was supposed to answer. *I'm gay* would be the most honest answer. *Marry me* was also begging to be typed.

Cassie: They look very good.

That seemed neutral enough.

Diana: You know, Cassie, you really need some nice jeans.

Diana: Every time I've seen you you're wearing a pencil skirt!

Cassie: They're appropriate for my job.

Diana: What about when you're not working? What do you wear?

Cassie: …the same things.

Cassie: It's not like I do much outside of working.

Diana: You better not be wearing a pencil skirt next time you visit.

Diana: Or, well, next time I visit you. All the visits are going to be in your house now, so I can take full advantage of your beautiful, amazing bathtub.

Cassandra remembered Diana in her bathroom: her skin wet and glistening, her hair slicked back from her face, an easy grin on her lips, and her body barely concealed by bubbles that were rapidly popping and revealing more and more.

This was going to kill her.

Diana: Though it's okay if you want to come here instead. I've still got a lot of food left from when my good friend Jimmy stopped by, so we could heat up some lasagna and get drunk on wine again.

Diana: No chance of Isabella storming in if she doesn't know where I live!

How tempting it was, even when the thought of keeping Diana from her bathtub seemed needlessly cruel. Who was Cassandra to not give Diana absolutely everything she wanted in life? Who was she to deny Diana the simple pleasure of going to

Cassandra's apartment, using her bathtub, and then putting on Cassandra's clothes?

Diana had taken the clothes with her, but that was fair. Cassandra hadn't returned the clothes Diana had given her the first day they saw each other, that day in the rain. Cassie wasn't going to give them back.

Cassie: If we're taking this away from the hypothetical and actually speaking about seeing each other again, then you may choose whatever you like, Diana.

Cassie: Isabella will not storm in if I stop ignoring her, and I know how much you enjoyed the bathtub.

Diana: Yeah, but you seemed so flustered. It's fine by me if you don't want to hang out naked in your bathroom or something.

Cassie covered her face with her hands again.

Cassie: I'm fine with it if you are, she sent, which was a big gay *lie*, since her hands were more or less shaking as she typed. Her face was in flames—why did Diana had to word it like *that? "Let's hang out naked!"* Good Lord.

Diana: Hey, maybe you can hop in. Do you think the bathtub could fit both of us? It'd be like old times!

The reminder of their sweet, sweet childhood wasn't enough to save Cassandra's mind conjuring up the images Diana seemed to be *begging* for her to imagine: the two of them in the tub, together; Diana would have her hair slicked back and her body would be all wet, glistening with the water and the bubbles, and it would all maybe start innocent—but when Cassandra kissed her, they would—

Cassie: Sure. But speaking of showers, I have to take one right now. I'll talk to you later.

She threw the phone on the bed and escaped to her bathroom before the conversation could spiral even more, her face on fire and her heart beating far too fast.

Chapter Seven

Diana grabbed her dirty greasy towel from the table and wiped her hands on it. She threw it over her shoulder and appraised the motorcycle standing in front of her. She set a hand on its handles and thought not for the first time about buying her own bike—but her budget wouldn't allow it, of course.

She was in a good mood. This had been an easy job and she loved working on bikes besides. She checked the hour. She still had to pack, since she was leaving to see Manuela tomorrow, but if she worked fast she could take a look at the car that had been brought in this morn—

Her thoughts were interrupted by the special ringtone she'd assigned to Cassandra. She smiled to herself. That had been the one thing lacking from her day: Cassie's beautiful voice.

She fished her phone out of her pocket.

"Hey, Cassie!" she said, sitting down at her stool. She let her eyes linger on the gleaming bike. "What's up? You're at work right now, aren't you?"

"Hello," Cassandra said, and Diana wasn't imagining the pleased note in her voice, was she? She grinned to herself. Cassie *liked* talking to her. "I know it's still eight, but I couldn't stand staying longer. I thought maybe, if you were also done with your day, we could have dinner?"

Diana felt her heart fill with joy.

"Yes!" she exclaimed. "Hell *yes*, Cassie! I'd love to see you before I leave! I'm so sad we won't see each other over the weekend, but I'm coming back Sunday night."

"You—you're travelling somewhere?"

Oh, oops. Diana hadn't mentioned it, apparently.

"I'm visiting Manuela," she told Cassie. "Just for the weekend. It's been some time since I've seen her."

"Oh," Cassie said. "I see. You hadn't mentioned it."

"Sorry, it just really slipped my mind. I haven't even packed yet!"

"Perhaps then it'd be best for me not to bother you," Cassandra murmured. "We can just have lunch on Monday."

Diana thought about Cassandra leaving work earlier so they could meet only for Diana to shoot her down and felt her heart constrict.

"No, no," she said, shaking her head even though Cassie couldn't see it, "let's go out somewhere, it's fine. I'm done with the day too and for packing I'll just throw some shirts and some trousers into a backpack, so it's all fine. What did you have in mind?"

"I…"

"You are no bother," Diana said very clearly, in case Cassandra had any doubts. Honestly, between Cassandra and Manuela, this kind of thing was getting tiring. "You could come here if you want. We can call for some pizza and watch some stupid TV."

Cassandra was quiet for a moment.

"Diana," she said, "how often in this week have you had pizza for dinner?"

Far too often.

"Don't ask questions if you don't *really* want to hear the answers," Diana said solemnly.

"You have to eat healthier, Diana."

"*You* have to eat a few more pizzas."

"…how about," Cassie tried, "you call for the pizza and I make a salad?"

"Well," Diana said, scratching her chin, "you're gonna have to bring the salad, because I've nothing to make salad with here."

Cassandra sighed, but Diana grinned because Cassandra sounded *fond.*

***

Manuela was four hours away by bus, which passed very quickly. The bus was comfortable and had Wi-Fi, so the hours passed by fast. She lived in a small town that was completely dedicated to the university where her sister studied.

Manny's building was old, made in red bricks. It was charming, the kind of building Diana would like to live in if she could ever force herself to live anywhere that wasn't a big city.

Manuela was standing by the open front door with her roommate by her side. She seemed to have somehow grown taller, or maybe just *fuller*: she'd shorn her pretty hair to her skull, she was wearing shorts with flip-flops, and her face was completely sunburned.

"Hi!" Diana shouted as she ran to her. Her longing hit her all at once and was instantly assuaged when she wrapped her arms like vices around her baby sister. This was Manuela, whom she'd raised, whom she loved more than anyone.

She was at college now—out of the house, officially out of the nest, but she was still Diana's. She hadn't let herself linger on it, but standing here with Manuela, so far away from home, the thought of going back to that empty apartment was *unbearable.*

"Hey, sis," Manny said to her hair, voice wobbly. "We speak to each other every day, what's all this enthusiasm about?"

"I *missed* you," Diana said, fervent, and leaned away so she could cup her face in her hands. "Christ, Manuela, you didn't tell me you'd shaved yourself bald like this!"

"It's a surprise!" Manny said, surreptitiously wiping tears from her eyes. "And I'm not bald. The hair is just very short—"

"I hope you're wearing hats," Diana said, sending her a playful look. "Wouldn't want to burn your giant bald head."

"Hey!"

"Hey, Diana," Manny's roommate Angela said, sounding bored. "Let's get in, I was in the middle of—"

"Come on, my sister just came home," Manny said, linking her arm with Diana's. "You can let go of your video games for a *second*, right?"

Angela sent her an unamused look.

"How about I make us some cake?" Diana said.

Angela brightened at once. Manny and Diana laughed and their smiles were exactly the same.

***

"How've you been?" Di asked, whisking eggs in a bowl. "I hope you cleaned up the place before I arrived, or else it's just rude."

Manny rolled her eyes, good-natured. She grabbed flour from a cupboard.

"Uh-huh, you say that as if your place isn't a dump."

"It's not a dump! If you keep saying those things, I'll leave you to go play whatever with Angela."

"No! If you start playing now you won't stop, and I want my cake."

"Aw, you know I don't have any video-games at home! *You*, however, can just search on the internet how to make a chocolate cake," Diana said with a shake of her head. "Speaking of something entirely unrelated," Diana said, dropping flour, sugar, and baking powder into the bowl with the eggs... "You saw I deposited some money for you? For the rent thing? You haven't said anything. I sure do hope you're keeping an eye in your bank account, Manny."

Manuela deflated all at once. She glared at Diana.

"I told you, you didn't need to."

"Are you really going to have this discussion again," Diana asked, bored, as she grabbed cocoa powder and butter.

"Yeah, because maybe if you didn't dump all your damn money on me, you'd *have* some kind of video-game in your house."

"I don't *need* video-games."

"Does anyone *need* video-games?" Manuela asked. She sat down on the counter beside where Diana was working. Diana eyed her, but it was Manny's house and so she couldn't say anything. "Just consider it, Di. Maybe buy yourself a new TV. Maybe buy yourself a shirt that isn't a dirty tank top."

"My tank tops aren't dirty!"

"You think I can't see the smudges on the one you're wearing because it's black? Think again."

"I don't care about my dirty tank tops," Diana said, waving the subject away. "I'm a mechanic, these things happen."

"Yeah, fine, you want to talk about money," Manuela said, annoyed. "Well, Di, I don't know how to tell you that I'm *an adult*, and that you don't need to keep giving me a damn allowance. I've got a job at the library here, you *know that—*"

"I also know it's not enough to pay for your books *and* your rent *and* the groceries *and* everything else," Diana interrupted. "Manny, you're nineteen, not *forty*, of course I'm still going to give you some money. Once you're done with college and you've got a job, and a place, and some security—"

"I am not *eleven* anymore," Manuela said firmly, hands curled in fists. She looked at Diana like she was willing her to *understand*—but the thing was that Diana understood far too well. "I'm not your responsibility anymore, you don't have to *shoulder me* anymore. I can get by on my own now, and you should buy yourself new clothes, a new TV, your fucking dream motorcycle. You—"

"I would have *killed*," Diana cut off, setting her spoon down forcefully, "to have this kind of safety net when I was your age, Manuela."

"I'm not you!" her sister shouted. "I don't have some little kid weighting me down, I'm free to spend my money how I want and *you're* finally free—"

"I'm not *free* of you, because you're *not a weight on my shoulders*," Diana shot back, her own hands curling. "I don't know how many *times* I have to say this, Manuela. I love you and I *want* to do this for you—"

"And meanwhile you live in an apartment a *third* the size of mine," her sister argued, "you don't have your bike, or even a crappy car, you don't have a good TV, or video-games, or a computer, your laptop is *ten years old*, your phone is new because *I bought it for you*—"

"I don't need those things!"

"But you *want* them," Manuela said, shaking her head. "You went to Cassandra's apartment to use her bathtub and you were so fucking excited about it— newsflash, Diana. If you didn't drop half your money in that stupid fucking college savings account, you could move to a place where you could have your own damn tub."

"I'm not moving out," Diana said, crossing her arms. "I live right above the shop, anywhere else wouldn't be as good."

"Yeah, see how you didn't mention anything else I said?" Manuela said. "It's because I'm *right.*"

"You're my *baby sister*," Diana said and turned back to her bowl, effectively ending the argument. "I'm still going to help you *pay your groceries.* You don't know what it's like to be desperate for money, Manuela. Count your fucking blessings."

"You're such an asshole about this," Manuela snapped.

Di didn't say anything. Manny walked out of the kitchen and plopped down on the couch beside her roommate. Diana sighed and rubbed a hand over her face. On the counter beside her, the phone buzzed with new texts, but she was distracted and didn't notice.

***

The three of them—Diana, her sister, and Angela—played basically every single game that the two of them had in the house. Angela got the cake from the oven and cut it in small pieces while Di made enough chocolate sauce and the three of them ate the cake like it was *fondue*. They played more games. Manuela fell asleep on her shoulder and Di forgot all about their stupid argument—she was just happy to be here.

Diana missed her sister like a limb sometimes, but at other times she was just glad she wasn't that much of a mother to her sister anymore.

At least a little bit.

Angela continued playing games and Di stopped, afraid that harsh arm movements would wake her sister up. Luckily, this made her free to pick her phone from her pocket and send Cassie a message!

She blinked at her phone. Cassandra had already messaged her *hours ago.*

Cassie: Hello. If amenable, please send text when you arrive safely at your sister's place.

Cassie: Diana?

Cassie: I'm choosing to believe you haven't read my earlier message and are not, in fact, ignoring me.

Cassie: Or worse, dead in a ditch somewhere.

Cassie: I hope she is well, too.

70

Cassie: I would like to meet her again, some day. She must not remember me, right?

Diana felt her face flush despite herself. Cassie had been worried about her, apparently, even if in a vague sense. Diana felt pleased that Cassandra had reached out to talk to her—as if she missed her.

Well, of course Cassie missed her. They were friends again. Diana would miss her like hell if she suddenly was gone away like this.

Diana: Hi! I'm sorry! I didn't mean to ignore you, I promise.

Diana: I arrived well, it's just a four hour trip. I baked a cake and we've just been playing video-games.

Diana: How're you? You're not working right now, are you?

Cassie: …I'm not.

Diana: D: !

Cassie: It's not like I had much else to do.

Diana: Oh, know what we could do? We could go watch a movie or something! We never did go to the movies, since we were too small to go alone and all when you left, but we can totally go now.

Diana: I mean, when I come back. On Monday, if you're free? Can you leave early again?

Cassie: I suppose we could go, yes.

Cassie: My siblings won't be too happy with it.

Diana: That's a plus for me, not something bad.

Cassie: Anyway, I'm glad you are well, and that she is, too.

Diana: I see that change in subject.

Diana: It's okay, though. We don't have to go or anything if you don't want to.

Cassie: I do want to.

Cassie: I wish you were here.

Cassie: We haven't seen each other in days and it's stupid to miss you on the one weekend you're out, but...

Diana rested her cheek on her sister's head and felt herself soften.

Diana: It's not stupid. I miss you too. We DO have fourteen years to catch up on.

Cassie: Yeah. But either way, I wouldn't want to keep you from your sister. Enjoy your trip.

Diana: I'll be back soon!

Cassie: I know.

Diana dropped her phone beside her on the bed and sighed. She'd hoped to stretch the conversation, but she knew Cassie "wouldn't want to be a bother"— no matter how much Diana insisted that she wanted to talk to her.

Chapter Eight

Cassandra turned off the screen of her work computer and started shuffling papers into her briefcase. It was Monday and Diana was back. It was six p.m. and Cassie had no reason to be here past this hour. She was going to leave and then go to Diana's shop, and they were going to go do something together. Honestly the idea of going out wasn't very appealing to her. Cassie would rather stay in Diana's home, on her couch, touching Diana from shoulder to knee.

She hadn't realized how much she'd missed Diana until she learned she was very far away, and somewhere Cassandra didn't know where to boot. Cassie had spent too many years not knowing where Diana was.

But Diana was home now.

"Hey," Gabriel said, lengthening the vowel, and tapped the door with his knuckles. "Hey, baby sis—oh, what's this? Are you leaving? What's up, Mike call you out to go somewhere?"

"No," Cassandra told him. "Nothing's happened. Did you need help with something, Gabriel?"

"Ah, yes. I don't know if you remember that meeting I had with our PR manager last week—"

"You didn't tell me about it."

"Ah, well, she asked me for a favor today and I *really* have no way to do it, so I thought, well, what better person to go to, right? And you're heading out already! So please stop by the—"

"I will be busy," Cassandra interrupted.

He paused, and stared at her. "Come again?"

"I will be busy," she repeated. She shrugged on one of her many boring, stupid coats and picked up her suit-case. "Apologies, Gabriel."

"...but—"

"Perhaps another day."

"Perhaps," Michaela said, leaning against Cassandra's door with an arm and effectively blocking her one way out, "you should stay here and help our brother."

Cassandra stared at her oldest sister. She hadn't noticed her there—hadn't seen her at all—and though she wanted to *leave*, the thought of having a confrontation with Michaela was enough to make her regret everything she'd done in her life to bring her to this moment.

She had that familiar tilt in the corner of her mouth. Like their entire family, always, Michaela was disappointed in her.

Stupid, passive, bland little Cassie, who'd never amount to anything.

"Michaela," Cassie said. She took a step back to allow her into the room, but her sister stayed where she was. "I hadn't seen you there. Was there something you wanted?"

"Yes, actually," she said. "Gabriel, run along now. My secretary can help you with what you want. I need to talk to Cassandra."

"Yeah, sure," he said, then fled.

Cassie stared at his retreating back and felt betrayed. How many times had she helped him with no questions asked this week alone, and he left her to the wolves with not a single glance?

Michaela walked into the room and closed the door behind herself. She gestured to Cassandra's chair as if inviting her to sit even if the office was *Cassandra's* and sat down on the armchair by the books in the corner of the room.

Cassandra set her bag down and sat down.

"Your behavior has been changing," Michaela started before Cassie could say anything. "And not for the best, Cassandra, which is a surprise to everyone. Not that we thought you'd get *better*—but truly, I did not think you could get worse."

That *hurt*—and it hurt like a fucking knife to her chest. So this was it, really, how they all thought of her—

And for once in her life, Cassandra grew angry.

"I'm one of your best employees," she said.

"Yes, and you'll never be anything other than that," her sister replied easily. "Therein lies the problem—and really it's not been the worst thing, it's very good for the company and for me to have someone as nice and dedicated as you. But you're not a *leader*, Cassandra, you're a simple employee, like you said, and now you're not even doing your duties properly."

Not doing her duties properly?

"I've not missed a single deadline," Cassandra told her, spine straightening up. "I haven't replied to an email a second late, I haven't denied help to any of our siblings when they asked—"

"Until now," Michaela cut off. She stood up. "I'm not going to fire you, Cassandra, you know that. Despite everything, you're my little sister. But I want you to pay close attention to my words: I am not happy with you. Put your bag down. Get your things. And get to work."

Cassandra stayed silent. Michaela gave her a look before she left, her pointed heels echoing behind her.

Cassie sat in her tiny, cramped office, coat on, bag to the side, completely alone.

***

Cassie waited ten minutes, grabbed her things, and left.

The walk to Diana's shop was short and Cassie made it in record time, clutching at her bag with white knuckles and irrationally afraid she'd bump into any of her many siblings or her siblings' acquaintances on the way. But no one saw her leave and no one saw her on the way. She pushed open the front door of the shop and visibly drooped in relief. She let out a long, stressed sigh.

"Oh, wow," Diana said. "You look like you had a stressful day."

Cassie looked up. Diana was lingering by the door that led to the garage, her hands dirty and her hair wild, and she looked absolutely beautiful. Her green eyes were shining and a grin was playing on her lips—no disappointment in sight, nothing in her expression that said she was anything other than happy at the fact that Cassandra was here.

"Hi," Cassandra said. The word was wholly inadequate to what she actually wanted to communicate: that she was glad to be here, too, that she didn't care about her siblings or her parents and that stupid fucking email she'd *still not answered* because it *really didn't matter*—but Diana stepped forward and wrapped her up in a tight hug, and seemed to understand anyway.

"Here, here," Diana murmured, petting her back. "Is everything all right, Cassie?"

"Just work," Cassie said, burying her face on her shoulder. "Um. Long time no see."

"Long time!" Diana drew back—but only a little, and didn't take her arms from around Cassie. "I'm glad you're early. I skipped lunch and I'm *so hungry.*"

"I have a feeling you skip lunch way too often," she said.

"Of course not," Diana said, waving a hand. She took a step back. Cassandra let her arms fall from her shoulders and immediately felt bereft. "So what do you want to do? I know we talked about going to the movies, but we could eat in, or go out to dinner, or do whatever you want. You don't really like to go out, right? So what did you have in mind?"

"Nothing," Cassandra's mouth said before she could stop it, "I just wanted to see you."

Diana looked at her with eyes just a bit wide. They were very green, Cassie couldn't help but notice for what felt like the hundredth time. Green was the rarest eye-color in the world.

"Oh," Di said, voice soft. "I... me too. I mean, I haven't thought of anything, either. I just wanted to see you too."

"... I see," Cassandra answered, awkward and awful, because she was a social disaster. She looked away, flustered. "I mean, I'm glad, since—"

Diana grabbed the lapels of her coat and hauled her down into a kiss.

Cassandra's brain came to a halt. The world froze. All she knew were the hands keeping her close and the lips around hers. They were very warm, full and pliant, and almost despite herself Cassandra found her arms wrapping themselves around Diana's waist. She was so small. Cassandra could envelop her entirely.

Diana let their lips slip from each other, just slightly enough that she could open her eyes to look at Cassie. That made their kiss something short and chaste, just a sweet little thing. Their first kiss.

"Um," Cassandra said.

"Well, that happened," Diana said lightly. She was peering up at Cassie with a curious expression and didn't seem nervous at all, even when Cassie herself felt like she was going to spontaneously combust where she stood.

"Yes, it happened," Cassandra repeated a bit dumbly.

It'd happened. She'd kissed Diana. Better yet: *Diana* had kissed her.

Diana had kissed her.

"You kissed me," Cassandra said, dazed.

"Yes, I kissed you," Diana answered.

Her face was all red, which made her green eyes glitter all the more. Cassandra was just so tired after this long day, her brain absolutely exhausted with her *entire life*—with her stupid long hair she didn't have the courage to cut, with the bland clothes she wore to work, the apartment she hadn't chose and *hated*, the parents who didn't give a *shit about her.*

There was so much she was tired about.

But Diana was bright and beautiful and lovely and she'd *kissed her.* Diana was the best woman in this entire planet and she wanted *Cassandra* out of everyone in the world, and Cassandra felt her chest fill with joy so bright it eclipsed all the rest of her stupid, miserable little life.

She yanked Diana back to her and kissed her with fervor bubbling from her lips—while delighted laughter bubbled from Diana's. Diana grabbed at her coat, at her hair, tugging it loose with a vengeance. Cassandra fit her hands around her waist, her hips, stepping forward until Diana hit her own table.

"God," she muttered, lips sliding wetly against Diana's, "I want to, just—"

"Oh, anything," Diana answered, curling her hands around fistfuls of Cassandra's coat to drag it *off* of her. "Whatever you want, Cassandra, I'm okay with *literally anything right now,* if only you let me get you out of these stupid fucking clothes—"

Cassandra hated them. She *hated them*, this stupid pressed white shirt and this black pencil skirt, her bland light pink coat and her stockings and her sensible little heels. Diana threw her coat at the floor and wrestled Cassandra's tie off of her and then threw it away too.

"Something tells me you don't like my clothing," Cassandra said.

Diana looked Cassie in the eyes. She grabbed her hands and set them on her own waist—on top of the hem of her shirt. Cassandra's fingers tightened over the fabric. Diana pressed a kiss against her lips and Cassie obediently lifted her shirt from her body.

It was as beautiful and muscled as Cassandra had expected. Her breasts were held by a dark grey sports bra and Diana looked absolutely *perfect* in it.

"They're not *you*," Diana whispered in the shell of Cassie's ear. She shivered. "You were *bright*. Your favorite color was *bright orange.* I don't like this sensible white shirt."

"Me neither," Cassie said, a bit choked, when Diana attacked her buttons and pushed the shirt off her shoulders to let it fall to the floor behind her.

Cassandra's bra was a small skin-colored thing and her cleavage certainly less impressive than Diana's, but Cassandra didn't have time to feel shy or ashamed—Diana looked up at her with eyes bright and hungry.

She wrapped her arms around Cassie's neck and pulled her down into another fervent kiss. Cassie pushed her forward and Diana leaned back against her desk, then hopped on top of it, on top of all the important papers strewn around. Cassandra pressed herself against her front—chest against chest, both of them absolutely glued together. Diana wrapped her legs around her.

"Oh," Diana said into her lips, "is this—is this going too fast? Do you care? I don't think I care."

Cassandra stepped away and knelt down by Diana. Diana's mouth dropped open and so did her legs, the motion automatic. Cassie looked up: this was a very good point of view, here on the ground, with Diana's thighs bracketing her, her stomach contracted in anticipation, her chest expanding rapidly with her panting breaths. Diana's face was flushed.

"I don't care either," Cassandra said, voice rough, and put her hands on Diana's thighs.

Di laughed, loud and delighted.

"Oh, man," she said, "oh *man*, Cassandra, you are full of surprises."

Cassandra kissed her stomach, tasting the salt in her sweat.

"*Christ*," Diana hissed, and slid a hand into Cassandra's hair.

Cassie kissed lower, under her belly-button until her lips hit the seam of her trousers. She popped open the button of her jeans—

"Oh," Cassandra said, surprised, looking down. "You're wearing your new tight jeans."

"Yeah, they make my legs look *great*," Diana answered, amused.

"They *do*," Cassie agreed, voice low, glad to finally be able to say it.

Her own face was beet-red, she knew, but for once she wasn't embarrassed or flustered. For once she knew exactly what she wanted, and knew she could have it.

She dragged the jeans down as far as she could before Diana stood and shimmied out of them, then out of her underwear, and leaned back on the desk again, bare before Cassandra except for that *fucking bra.* Cassie put her hands on her thighs and slid them slowly up her legs to her sides. She pressed a kiss against the place her thigh met her torso.

"Diana," she said, "will you take off that *goddamn* bra?"

Di laughed.

"How long have you been wanting to look at my boobs?" she asked, voice full of joy. "I bet you've wanted to touch them forever. You know, I should really have casually not worn a bra when we hung out, you'd probably have been seduced earlier."

Cassandra would complain about her use of the stupid word *seduce*, but she was seduced all right.

"Take *yours* off," Diana countered, but she was already reaching to take off her own. "You know, I know, I said I hated your clothes, but you look *so beautiful* right now, on your knees with just a skirt and some stockings."

Cassie felt herself flush even harder. She put a hand in her own cheek and felt it warm.

"Don't tease," she murmured.

"Damn, look at you," Diana whispered, setting a hand on top of Cassie's. "Look at that blush. I'd always wanted to see how far down it went."

Cassie kissed her palm, since they weren't really in a position that'd let her kiss her lips. She kissed the fine bones of her wrist, her veins, then held her hand with her own so she could drop her lips to her body. Diana leaned back in one arm, loose and nice, and Cassandra kissed down until her chin brushed against hair.

Cassie mouthed at her mound and Diana sighed in pleasure, leaning even farther back. She set a hand on Cassie's head, fingers carding through her hair, as Cassie parted her open with her fingers and licked her from as far back as she could reach right up to her clit.

"*Oh*," Di breathed out, fingers tightening around her hair.

Cassie wrapped her lips around Di's swelling clit and pressed her tongue against it, admiring her taste and loving her sounds. She squirmed where she knelt; her body was hot and she *wanted* to be touched, and to keep on touching. She dug her fingers into Diana's thighs. She slipped her tongue into Diana and licked at her—and above her Diana moaned, thighs contracting under Cassandra's hands.

She lifted a leg and hooked it over Cassie's shoulder, then pressed a heel against her back to bring her closer—which was just fine by Cassie, who was busy kissing at her and eliciting those sweet sounds. Diana wasn't shy at all, not even in this, and she didn't hold in her moans of pleasure. She rolled her hips against Cassandra's mouth, trying to get more pressure, more friction.

Cassandra took a hand from her thigh and pressed two fingers inside of Di. Diana let out a shaky breath and relaxed all at once, her legs growing loose around Cassie's head. Cassie lifted her lips to her clit again and wrapped them around it while she worked at her with her fingers—and when she crooked them and hit a spot *just so*—

"*Ah*, Cassie—"

—Diana came in a sweet release, her breath swooped out of her. Cassandra licked at her one more time and pressed her forehead against her stomach, and with a hand she lifted her own skirt, pushed down her stockings, absolutely dying for any kind of touch at all—

"Come here," Di said, voice rough, hands pulling at Cassandra's shoulders.

Cassandra lifted herself up wobbly, her knees protesting against the kneeling position. Diana pulled her into a lazy kiss and Cassie was about to burst from her own skin from sheer desire—

Diana began to kiss Cassandra on the lips as she slipped her fingers into Cassandra's underwear, and then into her. Cassie sighed shakily, hands clutching at Diana's shoulders, at her hair. Diana cupped her and hugged her close. The skin-to-skin contact was the best thing Cassandra had felt in her entire life: her arms around Diana's shoulders, their chests against each other, their stomach's touching.

Diana slipped another finger into Cassandra and Cassie arched her back in pleasure, mouth falling open—she was powerless in Diana's arms, moaning despite herself. Di crooked her fingers and then shoved a thigh between Cassandra's and the pressure, the friction, it was all too much and just *perfect* all at once—

Diana held her as she came, face buried in her shoulder and hands clutching at her short blond hair. Diana rubbed a hand over her back, soothing, and kissed her cheek, her jaw, her ear, until Cassandra finally relaxed in her arms.

She drooped all at once, but it was fine even though she was so much taller than Diana: Di was stocky and strong and held her with no problem.

"Hey," Diana whispered.

Cassandra didn't say anything, rubbing her face against her shoulder like a cat. Diana laughed, low and amused and loving, and didn't stop rubbing her back. It was as if she knew Cassandra sometimes just needed a moment to compose herself, as if she knew Cassandra wanted to bask in the moment just for a second.

And she did know, because she was Diana and she knew Cassandra.

"Hi," she murmured eventually.

She let go of Diana and took a step back to look at her—and what a funny picture the two of them made. Diana was completely naked and Cassandra had her skirt bunched up and her stockings bunched *down*, and they were still in the corner of Diana's dirty little garage.

Diana smiled at her like she was the *sun*, like she hadn't imagined ever being this happy, and Cassandra's heart melted. Di framed her hips with her hands.

"Hey, stud," she said, voice comically low. "I don't feel like going out to the movies or anything."

"Me neither," Cassie murmured. "Let's just order a pizza, and next time I'll bring something healthy for you to eat."

"Next time," Diana repeated with a grin.

Chapter Nine

Diana woke up the next morning feeling like the universe was smiling down on her. The sun was shining, the skies were clear, she stood up without muscle pains for once and took the longest, warmest shower of her life.

She nearly *danced* in the kitchen, she was so happy. She ate some fruit for breakfast and skipped steps down the stairway to her garage. It was early, she was feeling *so good*, she was going to *work* and *earn money* and then maybe buy Cassandra some *flowers*! And it was all going to be amazing!

Her phone rang. She picked it out of her back pocket and answered with a smile.

"Hello!"

"Well, somebody's happy," Jimmy said drily.

"I am!" Diana shouted into the phone. "Jimmy, my man! My most favorite friend! How are you? I hope you're doing wonderfully! When are you visiting? Jimmy, I miss you like a *limb.* I've so much to talk about!"

"So you finally asked that girl out?" he asked, gruff and amused. "I've *noticed.* You haven't sounded like this since…I think since Manny gave you the TV, years ago, after saving allowance money for something like two damn years."

"I have not in fact asked her out," Diana said brightly.

"So she asked you, big difference."

"Nah. We were going to go out or maybe stay in, but then we *kissed* before we could decide what to do, and then we had se—"

"*Don't tell me! I'm a grandfather I don't need to know these things!*" Jimmy shouted. "And anyway, changing the subject completely—"

Diana laughed.

"—what I actually *called to say* was, well…" He sighed. "I won't be able to visit you this week either, girl. My son scheduled a doctor's appointment right on Wednesday when I'd go, but then Thursday I'm going out with my wife and Friday is the grandkids' day. You know how it is."

"Oh," Diana said, and for the life of her didn't manage to hide the disappointment from her voice. She deflated like a balloon, her happiness flying out the window. "What doctor's appointment? Is everything all right?"

"Everything's just, fine, Diana. I don't need another worrywart next to me! You know how my heart is."

She narrowed her eyes, but there wasn't anything she could do.

"Well," she said, brightening her voice. "It's fine that you can't visit, I know how your family is, trying to hog you to themselves. Maybe next week?"

"Di, I'm so sorry," he apologized, gruff and sad. "You know I'd be there every day if I could. My legs just aren't the same—"

"I know, I know, it's fine," she was quick to reassure, even though her heart constricted when she thought about his rapidly deteriorating health.

But none of them had enough money to get him the meds he needed, so that was that.

"—and if one of the kids can't drive me there I just can't go alone—"

"I know, Jimmy, I don't blame you, really," she said. "Okay? You stay at home with your kids and your grandkids and come when you can, okay?"

"Hey, Di, none of that," he said. She could almost see him shaking his head. "I've a day for the grandkids and a day for *you* and they're equally important. I'll talk to my kids and see who can take me there—maybe on the weekend, if you're not too busy with your girlfriend."

Diana found herself smiling, pleased.

"My *girlfriend*," she repeated. "But don't worry. I've still got some of your food left here. I make it last, you know how it is."

He sighed. "I fear for your future blood pressure."

"Aw, Jimmy! Cassie's already said she'll start badgering me into eating salad."

"Well, seems like this girl is good after all," Jimmy said appreciatively.

"Of course she's good!"

"I haven't met her yet, how would I know!" he complained. "She better be there whenever I visit again."

"Yeah," Diana said, looking down, "I'll be sure to call her, whenever you're here again."

***

Diana set to working on the car that had been brought in not long ago; it was giving her a bit of trouble, but more trouble meant more money, so she wasn't bothered. Her back started to hurt again, like it always did. She just needed a new mattress, and to maybe stop sleeping on the old bumpy couch so often.

Carl arrived a bit late, like usual, with two cups of steaming coffee. Her mood soared into happy once again.

The hours passed. Carl was up front dealing with clients or playing on his phone, Jimmy had already called, Cassandra was at work and Diana didn't want to text her in case she was doing something important, and Manuela was in class at this time.

Diana really needed to make more friends.

She sat back with a sigh and stretched her back. Manuela was a college student, maybe she was skipping!

She called her sister.

"Hey, Di," Manny said, "what's up?"

"Hey, young girl, why're you not in class?" Diana asked sternly, standing up.

"I'm gonna go ahead and point out that you're the one who called me during class," Manny said dryly.

"Yeah, I figured you were skipping. I trust you to know how much effort you need to put into your education."

Manuela groaned loudly and pointedly.

"Anyway, I'm just bored and lonely and I've got great news I couldn't wait to share!" Diana exclaimed. She sat down on her stool. "You won't *guess* what happened yesterday!"

"You finally kissed Cassandra," Manuela said promptly.

"Yes!" Diana said, throwing a hand up in victory. "*And—*"

"Then you banged. Jimmy called me to complain about your oversharing."

"Curse that man! I wanted to tell you myself. You all are a bunch of gossips."

"Angela says congrats."

"Don't tell your roommate!" Diana complained, but she was smiling wide enough to make her cheeks hurt. "That's embarrassing."

Manuela laughed. "You haven't got one ounce of shame in your body."

"True," Diana said with a grin. "But hey, Cassandra is the most beautiful, wonderful woman alive. What should I do, tell no one? Come on. I'm gonna tattoo it on my forehead."

"I'm glad you're happy," Manuela said softly.

"You know me, easy to please," Diana said. "Also, this car I'm working on I think will give me some trouble, which means I'll probably get a bit more money, and your birthday is coming! What do you want, now I can get you something a bit better? I remember you swooning over that new phone. Do you still want that?"

"No, it's fine," Manuela said, voice growing more annoyed. "I don't want anything, Di, I've told you a thousand times."

"I'm not going to *not* give you a birthday present," Diana said. "What kind of sister would I be?"

"Hey, know what you can get me?" Manny asked. "You can, for my birthday, buy *yourself* a new phone."

Diana scoffed. "I don't need a new phone. This one works perfectly fine."

"Well, so does my phone. Guess you don't need to buy anything then."

Diana sighed, rubbing a hand over her face. "Manny, it's your damn birthday. Can we get the money talk out of the way and just—focus on the happy occasion? I can get you something sweet, something good instead of some cheap garbage for once."

"You *know* how I feel about you buying me something *sweet and good* while your fridge is a patchwork piece of shit Jimmy gave us seven years ago," Manny retorted. "Buy yourself something sweet. Okay, Diana? For my birthday, nothing would make me happier than seeing *you* with something you want. Okay? I've to go now, I have class. Bye, sis."

She hung up. Diana scowled down at her phone.

She wanted to buy something for her sister and nothing was going to stop her—but at the same time she knew Manuela would be pissed if Diana just disregarded all she'd said. Diana sighed. Maybe she could buy Manny that phone and then get some phone second-hand for herself so her sister wouldn't bother her too much.

Diana really didn't care about having a new phone. And her fridge worked just fine!

She threw her phone down and went back to work.

****

She finished late, with no reason to stop earlier than nine p.m. She was exhausted and dirty by the time she dragged her body up the stairs to take a shower. She threw herself on the couch and turned on the TV. She absolutely wasn't going to go to the kitchen and cook something up and didn't want to get take out again… She probably had some frozen whatever in her freezer that she could just pop into the microwave.

She turned on her TV and thought she'd do that in a minute, fully aware that she was probably going to fall asleep there and forget all about dinner.

She wondered what Cassie was doing right then and there…

Diana: Hey, Cassie? Are you free right now?

Cassie: Hello, Diana. I'm still at work, but I think I'll be heading home soon.

Cassie: Did you want to meet again?

Diana: Oh, it's a bit late. I just wanted to talk to you. I thought you were going to start leaving work earlier…?

Cassandra: Ah, well… Michaela complained about my current behavior and how lacking she finds it. I thought it'd be safer to stay until later today, since I slacked yesterday.

Diana frowned at her screen.

Diana: You didn't SLACK yesterday. You just left at the time you're actually SUPPOSED to leave.

Diana: Are you too busy for a phone call?

Cassandra: Not at all.

Diana called her. The phone only rang once before Cassie answered it.

"Hello," she said, voice low. Diana could hear the smile in her voice and smiled in turn. "Is everything okay?"

"Yeah," Diana reassured, "I just wanted to hear your voice. I'm here, so tired, all alone on my couch…"

There was a pause.

"I *could* stop by," Cassie said, a bit hesitant. "You know the company is very close to your shop. And we… we should talk about yesterday."

"Yeah, we should *talk*," Diana said, voice sultry.

"No, I—*Diana*," Cassie scolded, flustered. "I mean actually talk. Yesterday we just… ate, then I left, but… this is the kind of stuff we should talk about."

Diana didn't see much to talk about, but she also wasn't going to go around denying Cassandra anything she wanted in the world, ever, especially when Cassie wanted to *come visit her*.

"Bring dinner!" Diana said, stretching out on the couch.

"…were you not going to eat if I weren't coming there with food?"

"Of course I was," Diana lied. "But come quickly, I'm tired and hungry."

"All right," Cassandra said. "I'll get there soon. Don't fall asleep before I arrive."

"I won't," Diana lied again.

***

She woke up with Cassie's fingers carding through her hair, warm but uncomfortable, her back aching.

"Hi," Cassie said, low and shy.

"Hey," Diana answered, straightening up with a pained groan to land a kiss on Cassandra's chapped lips.

Cassie melted against her, kissing her back gently. She set a hand on Diana's cheek like she thought she was precious and was afraid of touching her too harshly.

"I've got some food for you," she said. "it's *not* pizza. You're welcome."

Diana just grinned at her and accepted the plate Cassie gave her. She scooted back on the couch and Cassie sat down beside her, the two of them touching from shoulder to knee. It wasn't really enough contact, but it'd have to do until they were done eating and could lay down on top of each other on the couch.

"What's this?" Diana asked, lifting the plate to take a better look at it. It smelled *amazing.*

"It's eggplant lasagna," Cassie said. "I had some leftovers."

Diana sent her a baffled look. "*Eggplant* lasagna?"

"Just try it," Cassie said.

It was amazing.

"See?" Cassie asked, lifting her eyebrows. "Food doesn't need to lack vegetables entirely to be tasty."

"I'll eat any vegetables as long as you're bringing them here."

"Lazy."

"Nah," Diana said, sending her a grin. "Just an excuse to see you."

A pretty blush rose to Cassandra's face—and actually, now that Diana was more woken up, she realized Cassandra had taken her coat and her heels off but still had her hair up in that tight bun. Not that she wasn't beautiful, but she was so, so lovely with her hair loose, and Diana really didn't like the sight of Cassandra so made up when she was supposed to be comfortable and at home.

"Hey," Di said. "You don't have to if you don't want to—but isn't that bun giving you a headache? Why don't you ever let down your hair?"

Cassie really should let it down, stop covering her freckles, start using more comfortable clothing. Diana didn't like how tight and uneasy Cassie looked in those clothes, always sitting absolutely straight as if afraid someone would come check in on her posture.

"I could," Cassie allowed, looking away. "I don't like my hair. It…it does give me headaches. But I really dislike it."

"Oh. Maybe you could get a different haircut?"

Cassie grimaced.

"Aw, sorry," Diana said. "But if it's worth anything, Cassie, I love your hair."

"You've seen it down *once*," Cassie retorted, rolling her eyes.

"It was a very special occasion!"

Cassandra blushed again, looking down.

"I wish I could just cut it all off," she admitted as if to a secret, putting a hand over her eyes. "I daydream about it sometimes, about just shaving it off, or getting a pixie cut. I just can't—"

Diana imagined Cassandra with very short hair and her heart burst.

"Oh, God," she said, "Cassie, please cut your hair. Please. I didn't think you could get even more beautiful, but now you've put this image in my head—"

"I can't just cut all my hair off," Cassie said, shaking her head. "And—I didn't want to talk about that." She looked at Diana's eyes very seriously. "I wanted to talk about yesterday, and what it meant."

"It means we're together now, right?" Diana asked, taking another bite of her weird but tasty lasagna. "Or at least we will be? We can go on dates and kiss a lot, it's going to be great."

Cassandra looked at her for a second.

"I… yes," she said, a bit awkward. "Basically."

Diana grinned at her.

"I don't understand how things are so easy for you," Cassie said, shaking her head. She looked down at her plate. "It all seemed so complicated and awkward to me."

Diana looked at her for a moment. Cassie was a serious kind of person; she wouldn't want her to think she wasn't being serious about this too. She put her plate on her tiny coffee table in front of the couch and grasped one of Cassie's hands in between her own.

"It's not really *easy*," Diana told her, "but that doesn't mean it can't be simple. I *really* like you, Cassie, and I think you like me, and yesterday was amazing, and I'd love to see where it can go. I told you—remember? That I was glad we'd found each other even if we ended up not liking each other that much?"

"Yeah," Cassie said, voice low but eyes shining.

"Well, we ended up liking each other after all," Di said with a grin. "That can just be that, if we want. I'm not gonna ask you to marry me right now or anything. Let's go on a proper date somewhen, okay?"

"Okay," Cassie said, bashful.

"*And*," Diana added playfully, "maybe, if your girlfriend asks nicely, you'll let down your hair? And maybe take off that make up so I can see your beautiful freckles?"

Cassie sighed, but she was smiling fondly at her.

Chapter Ten

Cassandra fled from work as she had been prone to doing these days: with her head down, hoping absolutely no one would notice her going. As usual, no one did; although it was rare—or at least used to be rare—that Cassandra would go home early, she'd always often go out to run errands for all of her siblings.

Not that she had been doing that much these days.

She walked over to the nearby sushi restaurant and only waited a few minutes before she was seated at a two-person table. There was no real reason for her to be anxious about this, Cassie reasoned with herself. She was just out during her *lunch hour.*

Isabella arrived quickly too, coming from God knew where. Cassie remembered Michaela's disappointment with her, who never did anything wrong, and how she'd never uttered a single word to Isabella.

They hugged.

"Hey, Cass!" Bella said, sitting in front of her. "Can't believe you asked me to lunch again, we had lunch together a few days ago!"

"Oh," Cassie said. She really had been making more of an effort with Isabella these days, but she hadn't really expected her sister to care much. "I just wanted to see you. It felt like we just saw each other when you burst angrily into my apartment late at night, so now I'm trying to fix that."

"Well, now you've been glued to your phone, so you haven't been ignoring me anymore," Bella said, sending her a small smile. "My life lacks excitement now. What am I gonna do without my twice-weekly heart attacks?"

Cassie rolled her eyes.

"Just place your order," Cassie said as if she didn't know exactly what Isabella was going to ask for. "They're serving yakisoba now, so I'm getting that."

"Oh, you eat yakisoba now?" Bella eyed her over the menu. "You've been more sociable and now you're trying new things. What's going on?"

"I'm dating Diana," Cassandra blurted out, then winced at her own words.

"Oh," Isabella said.

They looked at each other and Cassandra couldn't bear it and turned her eyes to her own menu.

"I mean," Isabella said awkwardly, "congrats? I guess that's why you've been different. I'd kind of suspected already, you know… but I still wish you'd told me sooner."

"It just—it just happened this Monday," Cassie said. "I went over and she kissed me, and—yeah."

She stopped, closing her mouth shut against all the words she wanted to say. Cassie didn't really have any friends and she didn't really get along *well* with anyone in their family besides Isabella and that meant that she was absolutely *exploding* with things to say— but she couldn't really say them to anyone.

She couldn't talk about her house, their parents, about Diana and her apartment and how beautiful she was and how lucky Cassandra was—she couldn't. Not even with Isabella, because Bella may support her but she still wasn't really comfortable with it.

"But, uh." Isabella cleared her throat. "I'm happy for you, Cass. You look happier these days."

"I am," Cassie told her.

Isabella looked down. "Then she makes you happy?" she asked, glancing up. "I'm glad you found her, and that you're together now. It'll be good for you, having someone, though I can't begin to imagine how you're going to tell everyone."

Cassandra stared at her, caught between two surprises: that Isabella was talking about Diana still and that she'd mentioned their family.

"Tell everyone?" Cassie said, dumbfounded. "I'm not telling anyone."

Isabella raised her eyebrows to her hairline.

"What do you mean, you're not telling anyone?" she asked. "Are you going to hide it? I mean, I understand why you would, no one knows you're… you know. But still, someone *someday* is going to see you with her. I thought you'd rather avoid the clusterfuck that *that* would be."

"I'm not telling anyone," Cassandra said. "Of course I'm not—they barely find me acceptable right *now*, imagine if they *knew*—"

"That's the saddest fucking thing I've ever heard," Bella said. "And you know I'm all for saying fuck our family and living like you want to live, but you've always been, you know, good."

Good, Cassandra thought, and snorted. *You've always been good*, Isabella said a breath after agreeing with Cassandra about their family found her barely acceptable as it was. It was comic, really, that none of Cassandra's efforts were for anything.

"They can make a… clusterfuck… about it if they want, if they find out," Cassandra said. "I'm certainly not starting anything. I don't owe them anything, much less Diana."

"Huh," Isabella said appreciatively, "you really have changed, at least a bit."

Maybe. Maybe this was just how she'd been all along, and she'd just been too alone to realize it.

***

Cassandra sat down on her desk chair heavily, already tired even though she still had several hours of work to go. Her conversation with Isabella weighed on her mind—she hadn't wanted to think about it, but her family was sure to find out about her sexuality and her girlfriend at some point, and it would not go well.

She wouldn't tell them, she couldn't, but at the same time the thought of *hiding* Diana as if she were something shameful was grating on her nerves. She made Cassandra so happy. She wished she could talk about her to *someone.*

"So, you're finally back," Michaela said from her doorway, looking almost curiously into the room. "I thought you wouldn't be, with your current track record."

"I was having lunch with Isabella," Cassandra told her blandly.

Remember Isabella? Cassie wanted to ask. *Our youngest sister? She never shows up and never does work at all and yet you never call her a piece of shit.*

Not that Michaela had called Cassandra that, but that was the feeling she'd expressed.

"Good to know," Michaela said, pointedly bored, and left.

Cassandra sighed. She turned on the screen of her computer and opened the file she'd been working on before—

"Hey," Gabriel said, knocking on her door a second after he'd *already entered* the room. "Are you busy? No? Good."

Cassandra watched dumbly as he made his way to the armchair in the corner of her room and sprawled on it as if he owned it, one dirty shoe up on the cushion.

"Sure," Cassandra said. "What do you need?"

"So," he said, scratching at his cheek. He looked around the room with interest, as if there were anything of importance in its bare walls, instead of looking *at Cassandra.* "I mean, I do need a thing—I've got some emails, and actually Mike wanted you to help Margaret with the minutes—"

"Of course," Cassandra said. Why wouldn't she help *Mike's* stupid secretary?

"But! What I actually came here to say before, uh, before Mike could stretch you taut and flay you alive is, uh, that, you haven't answered our parents' email yet, and—"

Cassandra's sigh *nearly* escaped her. She didn't *care* about that stupid bland email and *neither did her parents.*

"—you know how it is, they mentioned it to Mike, and I really wouldn't bother, wouldn't want to keep you from your work, but, uh, I know how you are with... our family, and stuff, so I wanted to warn you that *since you didn't answer the email* and thus our parents couldn't send you another one—"

Yeah, they *couldn't.* They just didn't *want to.* She kept silent.

"—then, uh, the thing that Mike wanted to come here to rub in your face and that our parents would *have told you* if you'd answered their email—"

"Gabriel," she interrupted. "Please, get to your point."

"Yeah," he agreed, nodding so vigorously all his too-long hair went bobbing along. "So, they're coming to town next week and they're staying in the apartment right above yours."

All at once her heart filled with dread.

"Oh," she managed. "I… see."

"Yeah," he said, sent her a finger-gun, then bolted out of the room. She stared at his back, then at her closed door.

That… that had been Gabriel trying to be considerate, she realized with a start. He knew the news would upset her and tried, in his own stupid way, to soften the blow. He… he'd been right that this would have been a thousand times worse if Michaela had been the messenger.

She didn't know what to make of it, so she stopped thinking about it and instead focused on the fact that *her parents were coming to town and they were going to stay in the apartment above hers.*

They'd basically have access to her *all the time.* They weren't—they weren't *bad people*, they were just callous and a bit uncaring, especially now that she was an adult, and they would be as demanding as her siblings when it came to asking her for things and they'd always side with Michaela, who was right now angry at Cassandra for leaving work—

Oh, Christ, Michaela was going to *tell them* she'd been underperforming. Cassie put her head in her hands.

She startled when there was a knock on the door. Michaela looked at her, eyebrows lifted.

"Margaret needs your help," she said. "Please, don't leave her waiting."

She left and didn't close the door behind her. Cassandra looked at her retreating back.

***

She arrived home and threw herself on the couch. She fell with a dull *thud* and her bag well to the floor just as dully. The last few hours of work had been hellish, and now when Cassandra thought about the future she could only think about how coming home would be hellish too, with her parents right above her.

She could stay longer at work to avoid coming home or she could flee to Diana's house, but there was no way to do that without them asking her *who*, exactly, she was visiting—and that wouldn't lead anywhere good.

Good Lord, how Cassandra missed Diana, even though they'd last seen each other only a few days before.

She let her arm slip from the couch and reached for her bag. She got her phone blindly and brought it up to her face.

Cassandra: Hi, she sent. *How're you?*

When Diana didn't answer back right away, Cassandra let her phone slip to the bed and sighed. She was tired and she wanted a shower and to eat something and she wanted to not get up from this wretched couch ever again. What wouldn't she do to be with Diana's in her tiny apartment, which was better than Cassandra's in no way whatsoever—except for the fact that Diana was always there.

Her phone buzzed.

Diana: Hey!!! I'm doing just fine! I'm at home, heating up the last of Jimmy's spaghetti.

Diana: I'd hoped to have more by now, but he couldn't come this week. His damned family really doesn't like me. How're you?

Diana: Do you miss me? ;)

Cassandra smiled, looking at that winking smile.

Cassandra: I wish I were there with you, she sent. *I just got back from work. It was a horrible day.*

Diana: Did something happen?

Cassandra chewed on her lower lip. But in the end—funnily enough, Diana already *knew* her parents from those fourteen years ago, and already disliked them. It brought a smile to Cassandra's face.

Cassandra: Gabriel told me our parents are coming back to town THIS WEEKEND and that they will be staying in their apartment above the one I live in.

Diana: Oh, boy.

Diana: That SUCKS. Come stay with me until they leave again!

Cassandra buried her face in her cushions to hide her blush.

Cassandra: I can't, if I'm living somewhere else they'll ask questions, and...

Cassandra: I don't want to open that can of worms.

Diana: Oh.

Her phone started ringing. Cassandra blinked at it, surprised, and sat up on the couch.

"Hello?"

"Hey, Cassie," Diana said easily. "Sorry, I thought maybe we shouldn't have this conversation through texts, I know how serious you are about this kind of stuff. So, when you said you didn't want to open this can of worms, what did you mean, exactly?"

Cassandra stood up and walked to the kitchen.

"I... they don't know I'm not straight and they certainly don't know about *you*—and I don't intend on telling them any time soon," she said. She opened her fridge and grabbed some eggs and the butter. Scrambled eggs for dinner, yay. "They're out of town nine times out of ten anyway, so it's not like it matters much, and it'd only create problems."

Diana was quiet for a moment.

"Yeah," she said. "That makes sense. I just..."

Cassandra set her frying pan on the counter and clutched her phone tighter.

"What?"

"Well, I know how you are with your family. I'm thinking—you don't want to tell anyone, do you?"

"...no," Cassandra said. "It'll only create problems and none of them actually care about me."

"Huh."

"...Diana?" Cassie tried, hesitant. "What is it?"

"Well... you know how my parents are, uh, dead, and I basically have no family outside my baby sister and this one friend?"

"Yes?"

"It's important to me," Diana said, voice gentle. "I... I don't really want you to hide our relationship because it'd be too much of a bother to work through the problems it'd bring, sure, but most of all—I don't have a family to *tell*, Cassie. I know you say none of them care and that we all hate your parents, but... but it's important to me."

Oh, Cassandra thought, and felt like someone had taken a knife to her chest.

"I..." she tried. "I hadn't thought of that."

"Yeah, I figured. I'm not telling you that we *have* to shout from the rooftops *today*, but keep it in mind, okay, Cassie?"

"Yeah," Cassie said, feeling awkward and stupid and thoughtless.

How could she *forget*? How could she not think about it? She hadn't wondered what Diana would want at all—she hadn't thought of her opinions, and of course it was *Cassandra's* family, but it was Cassandra *and Diana's* relationship.

She felt so inadequate.

"I'm an awful girlfriend," she whispered. "I'm so sorry, Diana. I hadn't thought of this at all."

"You're not awful, don't say that," Diana complained, and all at once her voice brightened. "But hey, can you imagine the look in your parents' faces when you show up with me on your arm? Like *Yes*

Mother and Father this is in fact my gay lesbian girlfriend, Diana Kress—yes it's my childhood friend, so glad you remembered!"

Cassandra snorted despite herself.

"I'm sad to disappoint, Di, but their faces really wouldn't change. The homophobia would be felt in their little *comments* and how they *acted* and how they treat me after, and it's going to be awful, even *more awful* because they already barely talk to me—"

"Hey, hey," Diana said, soothing, "Cassie—"

Cassandra rubbed a hand over her face.

"I'm sorry," she said, "I'm sorry about that. I'm—I have a weird relationship with my parents, it's... it's complicated."

"Hey, I'm here for you," Diana said, voice firm. "You can tell me anything, okay? If you want to talk— or if you don't. Everything's all right."

Cassandra felt wetness on her hand and was surprised to find there were tears in her eyes, sliding down her cheek.

"I—" she said, a bit choked. "There's nothing— there's nothing to say, Di. They don't care about me, they never *have*, it's just that I'm an adult now and they're not obligated to take care of me anymore so it's just... nothing. They're strangers to me," she said, voice hollow. "They don't care."

"Christ," Diana said. "I wish I were there to hug you. Cassie, I'm so sorry. That's... that's awful. I don't know what to say."

Cassie wiped her tears off her face and picked her frying pan back up. Time to make some eggs and to forget all this.

"It's fine," she said. "I mean—I *am* an adult, and it's been years, it's…"

"They're your *parents*," Diana said. Cassie could picture her serious expression, the way she'd shake her head. "And they're assholes, but of course it matters, of course you're hurt by it. Okay? What you're feeling is completely valid, Cassie."

She choked on a sob.

"Di, I really—really just want to make some eggs right now," she managed.

"Okay," Di said, easy and nice. "Okay. Hey, are you making an omelet? Now I feel like eating some eggs, but I don't think I even *have* any."

"How can you not have eggs in your fridge?" Cassie asked, baffled.

"Do you really doubt it?"

"…no. Of course you don't have eggs. I'll bring you some, okay?"

"Yeah, sure! How about tomorrow, during lunch?"

Cassie bit her lower lip.

"We'd only see each other for an hour," she said softly. "So maybe dinner?"

"Okay," Diana said, fond. "Dinner, then."

Chapter Eleven

Diana stared at the rows and rows of brands of rice.

"How the *fuck* am I supposed to know which one to buy?" she asked, incredulous. "This supermarket is a nightmare. I should have passed by Joe's shop, at least there I know—"

"You're the one who wanted to make your girlfriend shrimp risotto!" Manuela exclaimed, though Diana could hear in her voice how amused she was. "You think Joe's shop would have *shrimp*, huh? Or even rice?"

"No, but you didn't have to lead me to this huge supermarket that I didn't even know existed! Now tell me which brand to buy."

Manuela sighed and did as she was told. Diana bought what she needed for the risotto and a few other things as well—some chocolate, some bread, some cheddar cheese she'd been craving. She didn't really have the money to splurge, but Cassandra had sounded *so upset* the day before...

Manuela guided her as she went—less because she really *needed* her help and more because any excuse to talk to her sister was a good one. She went home with her phone in her pocket and Manuela still chattering to her on her earbuds.

"Hey, actually," Manuela said when Di was almost home, "have you spoken to Jimmy these days?"

"Oh, like, once after that one call where he said he wouldn't be able to visit. Why?"

"Well... you know he couldn't go because they scheduled a doc's appointment that Wednesday? And, you know, I call Jimmy more often just because I don't see him in person anymore so I've spoken to him more since then and—"

Diana pushed open her front door and waved at Carl.

"—the doctor prescribed this super expensive medication that he has to take *daily* and a new batch of exams for the next couple of months and Jimmy didn't *say anything*, but—"

"*What?*" Diana said, letting her plastic bags fall to her counter. She gripped at her phone. "Did something go wrong?"

"No, it's just… he hasn't said anything, but I'm about two hundred percent sure he just plain can't afford it."

"Oh," Diana said, stunned.

Although, of course, it made sense. Jimmy's children weren't rich by any extent of the word and the two of them had had four kids each, of course there was no leftover money at the end of the month. Jimmy had never taken the *best* meds in the world, always having to go for the ones they all could afford…

"I see," Diana said. "I'll… I'll give him a call."

"Yeah," Manny said, relieved. "You do that, please."

***

"Hey, Jimmy, my main man!" Diana exclaimed into her phone, wiping her dirty rag across her forehead. She was tired and aching and what better thing to do during her break than to call Jimmy like she'd promised? "How are you? I haven't spoken to you in so long!"

"Hey, Lady Di," he said, gruff and fond, and by the use of her old little nickname she knew that he was pleased she'd called him. "Why're you calling, girl, what's up?"

"Well, it occurred to me that I never asked you how your doc's appointment went!" she said brightly, sitting down on her rocky stool. "Also, I just missed you," she said softly.

There was a pause. Diana could nearly *see* Jimmy narrowing his eyes.

"You spoke to Manuela," he accused.

"She's my baby sister, I speak to her all the time," Diana said easily.

"About my appointment. What did she tell you?"

"Mostly that you have a bunch of expensive meds and expensive exams to pay for," Diana admitted. "How're you holding up? Is everything all right?"

"Everything's as fine as it can be," he told her gruffly. "Don't worry, Diana, I've enough people all over me about this kind of stuff! And anyway it's not like you have a pile of money to hand over, do you?"

"No," Diana said, "but I've a *little bit* of money to hand over, if that will help! You know I love you, Jimmy, I wouldn't do anything less than the best I can."

"I know," he said, touched. "But I'm okay, girl, don't you worry about me. My kids will figure it out— they're thinking about changing my health insurance to another company, if they can, but it's all so complicated, especially with all my problems... But anyway, forget that. How're you?"

"I'm just fine!" she said, leaning back on her desk. "I'm on a break during work and then later I'm making risotto for Cassie. She's been sad these days, family stuff, you know how it is."

"Oh, I know how it is," he said. "And speaking of—I'm visiting next Monday! So you're finally going to eat *actual food* for once."

"I just told you I'm doing risotto!"

"Yeah, for your girl!"

"Good Lord, Jimmy, I don't even remember what day it is today," Di admitted, shaking her head. "I'll be waiting with bated breath, though! Promise!"

"Hell, you are a mess," Jimmy said, absurdly fond.

***

To Carl's endless surprise, Diana actually finished working at a normal hour—around six in the afternoon—so she could go upstairs and start cooking Cassie's food before she arrived. Diana stood in her tiny kitchen with barely an idea of what she had to do, but she had bought what she needed and had a nice recipe on her phone and it would have to do.

Should be easy, really.

She prepped all she could, then went to take a shower, then went back to finish it all up—and all in all it all didn't take long at all. It was very easy, actually, and even fun.

Maybe Diana should cook more. The risotto seemed *delicious.*

She made two plates and covered them so they wouldn't get too cold before Cassie arrived. She tidied up her living room as best she could then sat, waiting for Cassie to arrive.

After a few minutes, Diana heard a somewhat shy: *"Diana?"* coming from downstairs and went running down the stairs.

Cassie was standing with just a foot inside the garage, unsure, and Diana realized she'd probably never entered the shop to find her anywhere that wasn't the garage and had to laugh. She caught Cassie by the hands and then drew her into a tight hug.

"Hey, love," Di murmured, "hey, how're you?"

Cassie melted against her.

"Hey," she whispered. She let go of her suitcase and let it fall to the floor to put her arms around Diana's waist. "I'm good. Just tired. You know how work is."

"Yeah," Di said gently, leaning back. She bent down to catch Cassie's suitcase and led her up the stairs.

Cassie sat down heavily on the couch and closed her eyes and didn't notice the two plates on the coffee table at all. Diana laughed, setting Cassie's case down wherever, and sat beside her with her legs curled up under her. Ugh, she thought, this stupid backache. Hopefully it'd pass later.

"Cassie," she said softly, smile lingering, "don't you want to take off those shoes, take off that coat?"

"I'm too tired," Cassie complained.

Diana had to laugh again.

"Come on, you can't sleep now! I made you dinner, Cassie." She picked up the two plates from the coffee table and set one on Cassie's lap. "You have to compliment me even if it's awful, it's my first time. I don't think that kitchen has seen cooking from me ever since Manuela moved away."

Cassie opened her eyes and looked down at the plate on her lap in surprise. A blush rose on her face and her expression softened all at once, lines disappearing from around her eyes.

"Oh, Diana," she said, voice soft, and turned to look at her.

"I know it's been hard, with your family and stuff," Diana said gently. "So I thought I'd do something nice for you. I don't know if you still like rice or shrimp, but. I hope you still do? I couldn't exactly ask."

"I love it," Cassandra said, reaching out for Di.

She drew her close and pressed a kiss to her lips, soft but firm. Diana shifted closer and let her lips linger, wanting the kiss to last longer.

"Thank you," Cassie whispered. "You don't know how much it means."

Diana grinned.

"Hey, we're in this together. I know your folks are arriving soon and you hate that they're staying right above you, but here is your home too, you know?"

"Yeah," Cassie said, eyes shining.

Chapter Twelve

All the seven McNara siblings went to the airport to receive their parents on that bright Saturday morning when they arrived from somewhere in Europe, Cassie hadn't bothered to learn. Although Cassie saw Michaela and Gabriel often at work and she was the closest to Isabella, the rebellious one, she didn't often see Iris, Henry, or Jamie, and it was more than awkward to stand in the busy airport with all of them.

They were mostly in silence. Isabella stuck to Cassie's side, bored, and the others made small-talk like strangers in an elevator.

Cassie kept her phone clutched in a hand and kept away from Michaela, but didn't move away from Gabriel once he came to stand next to her. They didn't say a word to each other.

Her parents were fashionably late, enough that Bella had grown tired of standing and had promptly sat down on the floor by Cassandra. She stood up once their mother's white halo of hair showed up among the crowd, shooting up before they could see her on the floor.

"Hello, kids!" their mother said, and they all chorused a *hello* back. "I've missed you all."

She went around hugging them by order of birth: first Michaela, then Henry, Gabriel, Iris, Jamie, Cassandra, then Isabella. Their father followed, hugging his daughters and giving his two sons pats on the back.

"I hope you all didn't wait too long," he said. His voice was low and soft; he was a man one just couldn't imagine ever shouting. "You know how planes are, of course they never take off or land on time."

"Of course," Michaela said. "It was no bother to wait, Dad. Come on, let's get away from this crowd. You two must be hungry."

"Ah, we are," their mother said, shaking her head. "I hate plane food, so I'm starving. Let's go home—did you remember to clean up the house before we arrived?"

"It's cleaned up and the fridge is stocked," Michaela said smoothly. She linked her arm with their mother and led all of them to the parking lot. "I've had my housekeeper go to your house and prepare an amazing lunch. It won't take long to get there."

"How nice," their father said, smiling nicely like he was smiling at a stranger—and there they went, the McNara parents with their hands wrapped around each other lovingly while they spoke to Michaela as if she were someone they'd hired to prepare their arrival home and not their eldest daughter, while the rest of them trailed behind unacknowledged and silent.

***

The ride home was long and awkward, at least to Cassandra. Isabella slept on her shoulder while she tried to ignore how uncomfortable being glued to Jamie made her feel. Michaela, Henry, and their parents went in Mike's car while Gabriel, Iris, Jamie, Cassie, and Bella went in Jamie's. No one spoke. The radio was too loud.

***

Michaela's housekeeper had indeed cooked up a feast for their parents' arrival, which was as useless as it was meaningless. Cassandra knew a lot of this food

117

would be thrown out, though Gabriel at least was sure to sneak some of it home. There was lunch proper, some rich kind of pasta with a creamy white sauce, but also salads, pastries, and snacks around.

Their apartment was exactly the same as Cassandra's. It was, for some reason, strangely satisfying to see it was as hollow and blandly decorated as hers.

She thought not for the first time of something Diana had told her: there was no reason she couldn't just move out.

They all sat down on the big dinner table that had been perfectly set. Their parents started including Henry in the conversation they were having with Michaela, which left the rest of them to munch on their food and make awkward small talk to each other.

Cassandra leaned back against Isabella's shoulder and ate her pasta. It was good.

She wished Diana could have some of it. Between all the pizza and lasagna she ate, it seemed a safe bet that she'd like pasta in general.

If anyone noticed Cassandra's odd silence, they didn't comment on it. Isabella sent her a somewhat worried look, but Cassie just shrugged and she let it be.

She was just tired of this dance. She was finding a lot of merit in Diana's easy-going attitude—if this was a farce, why should she contribute to it? They could complain to her if they thought badly of it, but she didn't want to do this anymore.

The afternoon went on. Although Cassie stood by her decision not to engage in the stupid small-talk with the people who were related to her but who were also all strangers, she didn't actually get her phone from her pocket to talk to Diana, because she wasn't stupid and didn't want Michaela or her parents to take notice.

So the time passed slowly.

They all kept on munching on pastries as the hours went on. They relocated to the living room. Their couch was stiff. Someone turned on the TV. Their mother spoke to Gabriel about the soap opera and Michaela spoke to their father about the company.

"—doing well this month," Michaela was saying. "I've implemented the changes you spoke about the last time you took a look at the files I sent you and things have been running more smoothly than ever."

"Good, good," their father said with a nod. He took a sip of his tiny cup of coffee. "And how've the girls been? I'd hoped Isabella would be heading toward manager of the publicity department by now…"

"Certainly not," Michaela said briskly. "The girl barely shows up at the building. I could not give her the necessary positions if my life depended on it."

Their father looked at Isabella sadly and his expression was *exactly the same as Michaela's*—he was sad and disappointed and resigned. Unlike Cassandra, whose chest was constricting with anxiety at the mere sight of that face even if it wasn't directed at her, Isabella rolled her eyes and took another bite of her croissant.

"What about you, Cassandra?" he asked, turning to Cassie when he saw her looking at him. "How have you been?"

Cassie had to keep in a laugh. The question was bland and unspecific, and that was because unlike the *problem child*, Isabella, their father hadn't had any plans for Cassandra at all, much less as the manager of anything.

"I've been well, Dad," she said in the same tone of voice as his. "I've been working as always."

"Well," Michaela said, taking a sip of her own coffee, "that's not exactly true."

Cassandra tensed. Their father turned a confused frown to his eldest daughter, because after all Cassandra never changed in anything, much less in regards to work.

"What do you mean?" their father asked. "I'm sure Cassandra hasn't slacked—it's *Cassandra*."

"But she has," Michaela said. She shook her head, nearly sad. "She's been leaving earlier and has even disappeared after her lunch hour. I don't know what's happening—but I suppose it was inevitable. No one is that predictable for so long."

Cassandra looked away when their father turned to her, focusing her eyes on the saucer on her lap, and tried not to even *picture* his expression—even though it was impossible, even though it was nearly *burned* into the insides of her eyelids. Cassandra was stupid and a disappointment and she could not stay in their father's presence for more than a day before he turned that expression to her.

"Really, Cassandra?" he asked, sad. "I'd hoped you'd get better, not worse. But I suppose Mike is right...though I'd always hoped for the best. Why have you been slacking?"

"It's not like you've anywhere else to be, or anyone else to be with," Michaela spoke into her cup, eyebrows lifted over the rims of her glasses.

"I have a girlfriend," Cassandra said.

Everyone froze.

The conversation halted. Eight pairs of eyes directed themselves to Cassandra, who had closed hers in sheer terror the second the words had left her mouth. But Cassandra had somewhere else to be and some*one* else to be with and she'd much, much rather be with Diana right now, so much she felt it like a physical pain in her chest.

"...what?" their mother asked, voice faint.

Isabella grabbed her hand. When Cassandra lifted her eyes, Bella looked horrified.

"I have a girlfriend," Cassandra repeated, willing her voice to be firm. "Her name's Diana Kress. I've been seeing her for some time now. So I have in fact been slacking—which means I've been going home at the time *my shift ends* instead of at ten p.m. at the earliest—because I want to see her."

"Oh, boy," Gabriel muttered.

"Wh—what?" Cassandra's mother said, stuttering for the first time in Cassie's memory. "You're..."

She covered her mouth with her hands, unable to continue. Her father sat like a stone. Isabella's nails were digging painfully into her skin, but Cassandra thought that if she let go she was going to keel over dead.

"Gay," she completed for her mother, voice blank. She wasn't gay, really, she was bisexual, but she knew the word didn't exist in her parents' vocabulary. This would have to do. It was what they'd think anyway, no matter what she said. "Apologies for destroying your visit home with this news. I truly hadn't meant to tell you at all, but in the end I'm not as immune to Michaela's poking as I'd wanted to be."

Her father stood up at once. His empty cup rolled to the floor, shattering loudly in the silence.

Cassandra stood up as well, utterly unable to hear any words he had to say—any swearing or any empty platitudes, it didn't matter which. Isabella stood with her, a fact which nearly made Cassandra sob.

"I'm leaving," she said. "I'm sorry, again. I can't stay here right now."

She walked out in silence, her baby sister glued to her back, and didn't once look back.

***

Cassandra walked as fast as she could on the street, one hand over her eyes so the strangers in the street wouldn't see the tears falling down her face. It'd be too humiliating, she thought, if anyone she knew were around and saw her like this. Isabella didn't utter a word, not even to complain about her harsh pace.

She got to Diana's shop and didn't look at Carl as she crossed the reception. She walked into the garage, which smelled like cars and oils and fumes and was dirty and dark and saw Diana sitting on a stool with her back curled like a question mark, her tongue between her teeth as she stared at the bike in front of her in concentration.

"Diana," Cassie said, voice rough and shaky.

Diana looked up at once. Her eyes widened when she caught sight of her expression of her white-knuckled grip on Isabella. She stood up.

"Oh, Cassandra," she said, voice as soft a feather, and Cassandra finally burst into tears.

Chapter Thirteen

Diana wrapped her arms around Cassandra and held her against her as she cried. Isabella stood behind her sister without letting go of her hand and looked at her with an odd expression on her face—like she'd never seen Cassandra cry, like she'd never expected to. Diana just closed her eyes and rubbed a hand up and down Cassie's back, trying to be as soothing as she could.

Cassandra's sobbing quickly tapered off, way sooner than Diana had expected.

"Oh," she said, "Diana, I made a mess of it. I didn't want to but—I have no idea what's going to *happen* now."

"Hey, it's okay," Diana murmured. "It's all fine. Let's go upstairs, you can wash your face and drink some water."

"Okay," Cassie said, eyes down.

Isabella waved awkwardly to Diana, who nodded at her. They went upstairs in a chain, Diana holding Cassie's hand holding Isabella's hand. She pushed the two sisters to the couch and hastily washed her hands, then got water for the two of them. She sat by Cassie, whose body automatically tipped toward her.

"What happened?" Di asked. "I know you were meeting your parents, but I really didn't expect this."

"No one did," Cassie said dryly, voice still a bit shaky.

"Yeah, uh," Isabella piped up when Cassandra didn't say anything after that, "Cass just outed herself to the entire family during our post-lunch coffee session and then ran out before anyone could say *literally* anything other than *what*."

Diana winced. "Oh."

"*Oh* all right," Cassie murmured. "My mother covered her mouth with her hands and my father—I don't know what he was going to say, but I just couldn't bear it. Even if he was supportive I knew it was all *fake*, it's all so stupid and—I just wanted to be here," she said, shoulders drawing in. "I didn't want to be in that place anymore."

"I'm glad you're here," Diana said softly. "We'll deal with this, okay? It's not the end of the world."

"I think," Cassie said, a bit dazed. "I think I'm going to cut my hair off."

"Oh," Diana said.

"What?" Isabella asked, baffled.

Cassandra laughed a bittersweet laugh. She looked up at Diana.

"It can't get worse than this, can it?" she asked, reaching out to grasp Diana's hand in a firm grip. "It can't get worse than this awful afternoon—and what do I care what they'll say if I cut off all my hair? Won't be worse than whatever they'll say after I outed myself like this. I might as well, right?"

"I'd put off doing anything that drastic right now," Diana told her, "but—I understand, Cassie. I get it."

"I don't," Isabella said, confused. "Since when do you want to *cut your hair off?*"

Cassie sighed.

"Bella," she said, "it's been *years*, let me tell you."

***

125

Diana disentangled her limbs from Cassie carefully enough that she didn't wake up and made her way to the living room. Cassandra, who'd been so stressed lately, deserved to sleep a bit, but Diana was too hyped up to do it, so she sat on her couch and got her phone from where she'd left it on the coffee table.

She dialed her sister's number.

"Hey, Manny," she greeted, voice low. "I hoped you weren't at a party or anything like that."

"It's afternoon, Diana," Manny said, a tone of voice like she thought Diana was being stupid. "Parties start at, like, ten p.m. What's up, did you need anything?"

"Just to talk," Diana said with a sigh, letting her head fall back to the back of the couch. "You know how Cassie's parents are back in town, and they just arrived today—"

"I didn't know!"

"Yeah, that's a thing. So the whole lot of siblings went to receive them and all and I'm not sure how exactly it went down, but Cassie basically outed herself to the entire family and then left before anyone could say anything."

"Oh, Christ."

"Yeah," Diana agreed with feeling. "She came here, but she's napping right now. Man, I don't know how her family *functions*, but I sure do want to punch some people right now. You ever seen Cassandra sobbing? *It's not fun.*"

"I'm sorry about that," Manny said, voice low. "Must have been awful. Remember when *you* came out?"

"I swear our parents didn't say a *word* to me for like a whole damn week afterwards."

"Yeah."

There was a pause.

"But I think they'd have been okay with it," Manny added, voice soft. "Eventually. They'd have been happy that you found Cassie again."

Diana laughed. "Damn, you don't remember, Manny, but they *loved her*. So yeah, we're... we're just going to try and deal with what comes out of this. With luck her whole damn family will just ignore it like they do with everything, but also I think that if that happens Cassie is going to spontaneously combust."

"Guess that'll be a fun thing to look forward to," Manny said dryly.

"Yeah. And—changing the subject—I called Jimmy, he's finally escaping the clutches of his evil children to visit me in two days!"

"Oh, awesome! Did you talk to him about his meds and stuff?"

Di winced. "Yeah, but he *really* didn't want to talk about it. He says his kids bother him enough about it. I really don't know what to do to help him, Manny. I've looked at my money—at my finances and stuff—but I think if he ever found out that I took money from my let's-expand-the-business-fund, he'll actually murder me."

There was a pause.

"But," Manny said, "there's another fund you could take money from."

Diana felt herself grow annoyed.

"Yeah, and next time you need new books, money for a school trip, or something like this rent thing happens again—what're you going to do, huh? What if something happens? What if an accident happens? I'm not taking money from your fund. Speaking of," she said, trying to change the subject, "I've sent your gift in the mail already, it should arrive this week."

She could hear Manuela taking about a thousand deep breaths on the other side of the line, and still when she spoke Diana could hear the undercurrent of anger in her voice.

"I'm not a kid anymore," she said. "I'm an adult now, Diana. I know you want to, but you *don't have to take care of me anymore*. I'm okay on my own, I really am. I promise. I have a job, I'm saving my own money for emergencies. It's been eight years since our parents died," she added, voice soft. "You've taken care of me well during this time, but you're my big sister. *You're not my mom.*"

Diana stared at her coffee table, stunned.

"I raised you," she said, shaking her head. Of course Manny was right, but—

"Yeah, but I was *eleven*, not a newborn," Manuela said. Diana could almost hear her rolling her eyes. "You get what I mean? It's not your responsibility to support me forever. You taught me well and I'm saving money and *I'll be all right.* Know who won't be all right? James Robert Price, our dear beloved friend, if he can't take the fucking meds his doctor prescribed."

Diana rubbed a hand over her face.

"Manuela—"

"No, this is non-negotiable," Manny interrupted. "I'm an adult and I get to make financial decisions regarding money you're saving for *me*, and I say you *give that money to Jimmy*."

She wanted to, Diana wanted to do that *more than anything*. Jimmy's health was a mishmash of a thousand little issues and he wasn't getting any younger—but of course her baby sister came first, always, no matter what.

But—

Manny was nineteen, not nine. Not anymore.

And Diana was her sister, not her mother.

Di covered her face with her hands and deflated all at once, a heavy weight suddenly not on her shoulders anymore. She didn't have *that much* money in the college savings, but it was *enough*—enough to help Jimmy, for sure, and maybe enough to give Diana the last couple of bucks she needed to feel safe enough to start thinking about expanding her business—

Yet her heart still constricted when she thought about leaving Manuela adrift.

"Go take a nap with your girlfriend," Manuela ordered, "and then call Jimmy—or maybe wait to surprise him during his visit. Okay?"

"Okay," Diana mumbled. "Okay, *fine*, Manuela. Fine. I'll give the money to Jimmy—"

"And buy yourself a new fucking fridge."

"*Baby steps*, Manny."

***

"Hey," Cassie murmured when Diana slipped into bed beside her. "Everything all right?"

129

Diana kissed her forehead. "Everything's just fine. I was just talking to Manuela. Little rascal finally convinced me to stop giving her money like a responsible big sister and just buy a new fridge or something."

"Oh, thank God," Cassie said with a sigh. She reached out and wrapped Diana up in her long arms, bringing her to her side. "Maybe a new TV, too?"

"Shut up," Diana said, pressing another kiss to her forehead. She swiped her hair back, admiring the faint freckles by her hairline. "I'm giving most of the money to Jimmy. His health's not the best and his family can't afford to buy the meds he needs."

"Oh," Cassie said. "That's very kind of you."

"We're family," Diana said with a shrug.

She slid her hands from Cassie's face to her neck, then to her shoulder, admiring how soft and comfortable she looked in one of Diana's sweaters instead of in one of those stupid white shirts she wore every day to work. She looked *absolutely beautiful* like this, sleepy on Diana's bed.

Cassie cupped her cheek in a hand and brought her down for a kiss. Their lips slid together wetly and with no hurry. Cassie's chapstick tasted like white chocolate, which made the kiss even more delicious.

Diana thought about how, despite Cassandra's earlier sentiments, she'd told her family after all, like Diana had told her was important for her. Maybe it hadn't had anything to do with Diana, whatever it was that made Cassandra blurt out her secret during a family meeting, but it still made Diana feel warm beyond measure.

She licked into Cassie's mouth and slid their legs together under the cover. Cassie sighed, tilting sideways until Diana was on top of her, arms bracketing her arms. She slipped a leg between Cassie's, appreciating her long bare legs even if she couldn't see them right then and there.

"You should wear tiny pajama shorts more often," Diana murmured.

Cassie huffed out a laugh. "I knew you hadn't given me these accidentally."

"Oh, no," Diana said with a grin. She arched her back and pressed her thigh *up* against Cassandra and Cassie let out a breathy moan. "This was no accident."

Cassie rolled her hips under her, pressing up against Diana's thigh, sweet and slow, and Diana leaned down for another kiss. Cassie clutched at her shoulder, her other hand buried in Diana's hair, and Diana wanted to do the same—to card her fingers through her hair, now she still could before Cassandra cut it all off, wanted to grab at her hand and not let go. But for now she rocked down against Cassie and swallowed her little moans with her kisses.

There was time for that later—there was time for everything later.

Cassie craned her neck to the side and Diana pressed her lips against the corner of her sharp jaw, then down to the tendons of her neck, pressing open-mouthed kisses against her skin. Cassie squirmed under her, searching for more friction, and Diana felt her body waking up everywhere they touched.

"Cassie," she said, strained, "can you please—"

—and Cassie lifted her own thigh where it rested between Diana's legs without another word, giving a breathy laugh when Diana whined at the contact. Di let her weight down on top of Cassie and moved her hands to her sides, slipping them under her own sweater to cup her small breasts in her hands.

Her own were so big and such a *handful*, but Cassie's were just perfect. She made a pleased sound low in her throat at Diana's touch—then whined when Diana pressed her fingers against her nipples until they hardened into nubs, utterly perfect against Diana's own skin. She pressed another kiss to her neck, smug that she *could*, that shy Cassandra was just letting her.

"Christ, Di," she breathed out. She curled a hand in a fist around Diana's hair and brought her up for a kiss, biting at her lower lip before sweeping her tongue over it.

"You're too cute," Diana murmured. "I can't help it."

Cassie just breathed out, didn't answer, moving an arm to cover her eyes with, to try and cover the blush that went down to her breasts and then beyond. She arched her back on the bed, rubbing herself more firmly against Diana, and moaned loudly.

It was just afternoon and the neighbors could probably hear them, but none of them could bring themselves to care.

They came together, Cassandra with a hand against her mouth and Diana with her mouth against her neck, their names muffled against skin. Diana pressed herself entirely against Cassie, content to lay on top of her, her weight anchoring her down into her bed. If only she could keep her here, she thought, if only Cassandra would stop going back to that stupid apartment she hated.

They relaxed slowly, growing loose around each other. Cassie uncovered her face to look at Diana, then flushed again at whatever look was on her face—one that was probably, Diana knew, of utter fondness.

It was more than fondness.

Diana cupped her face in a hand, sweeping her thumb over a mole.

"I love you," she whispered.

Cassie's face contorted like she wanted to cry—and a tear escaped one of her eyes, sliding down to her hair.

"I love you too," she said. "I do. Everything will be fine, won't it? Even with—even with everything. It'll be fine."

"Yeah," Diana told her. "We'll get through it together, you'll see. In the end it won't be so bad."

Chapter Fourteen

Cassandra woke up with the smell of bacon in the air and for a few long blissful moments as she made her way to Diana's kitchen she forgot everything that had happened the day before: the awkward reunion, her anger at her whole family's relationship with each other, and her coming out to everyone out of nowhere.

She hadn't had bacon, it felt, in *years.*

"Morning, sunshine," Isabella said, shoving a plateful of bacon with eggs at Cassandra. "Here, eat breakfast that isn't fruit for once, get some proper food in you. You're gonna need it."

Oh, that did not bode well.

Bella waved her off, so Cassandra sat down on the couch—where Diana was sitting curled, arms crossed over the arm of the couch, taking a nap. Cassandra's eyes lingered on her sleeping face: her pink eyelids and her pink mouth, the curve of her cheeks, her unmade eyebrows.

"She was apparently up for hours this night working out some money stuff," Bella called from the kitchen. "She conked out basically the *second* I walked in."

"I see," Cassie said softly.

Yesterday really had been a shit day, at least before she remembered how it ended.

Diana was right. Things would not be as bad as she feared and they would work it out together.

"So," Isabella said, sitting down beside her with her own plate of bacon and eggs, "I'm here to tell you what happened yesterday in our family—and yeah, don't grimace, Cass, you weren't even there to listen—and you won't like how it ends. Our parents want to see you later today."

Promptly Cassandra's tentatively good mood left her and a black hole installed itself in her chest.

"I see," she said, a bit choked.

Bella patted her shoulder. "Eat your food, sis. You really need to get some more protein in your diet. So! Gabe was the one who reached out to me and we got to talking about what happened. Apparently after we left—you know our parents—so obviously they had no idea how to act, and just started acting like nothing had happened. Which isn't so bad, right?"

Right, Cassandra thought, except the thought made her feel hollow. She really *had* imagined it as the best case scenario, that her parents would just pretend nothing had changed, but that would underline just how *little* she meant to them and...

It'd be unbearable.

"But, as you could expect, Mike was *pissed*," Bella continued. Cassie ate a strip of bacon. God, it was good. "Honestly, I think it's less because of the whole girlfriend thing and more because she *didn't know*, and also because, of course, Mike is her parents' daughter to the core and absolutely hated that you dropped this bomb on them and ruined the weekend."

"Yeah," Cassie said. She ate another strip of bacon.

Bella winced. "You—you know what I meant. I didn't mean to—"

'I know, Bella," Cassie said gently.

"…okay. Ruined their *plans* for the weekend. But yeah—then Gabe said, you know, it was really awkward for *everyone* but we're all used to dealing with bullshit from our parents, so that was that— except at one-point Mom just…set her cup down and started asking around."

"…asking?"

"About you," Bella said. "She asked Mike first, but she didn't know anything. She wanted to know if anyone had known, how long this had been going on, who this woman was—"

Cassie frowned. "But she's met her."

"I don't know, man. And yeah, they want to see you again today, presumably just for some coffee. I… I don't know if she was asking around because she realized she literally doesn't know anything about you, or because she was just wondering how many of us were in on the secret before she knew—I don't know, Cass. You know how Gabe is."

Gabe, Cassandra thought, and decided to focus on that for a second.

"I know," she said. "You said he was the one who reached out to you?"

She shrugged. "He seemed a bit worried. You know, Gabe has his moments, even if he's mostly just an ass 99% of the time."

"Yeah," Cassie said, looking down at her half-filled plate.

But he'd reached out.

***

To say her trip to her building was unbearable was to put it lightly; each step weighted

136

approximately a ton. Cassie went and panicked about showing up with the same clothes as yesterday before she remembered her own apartment was just under her parents'. Diana went with her, holding her hand easily and making small talk like she knew Cassie had to focus on something else.

She went up with Cassie to her apartment. Cassie took a shower and put on some presentable clothes and left Diana there with a kiss, promising to come fetch her so they could go back to Di's place the very *second* her parents let her go.

It was only a floor up to their apartment. Cassandra wiped sweaty palms against her skirt and took a deep breath.

She was surprised when Michaela opened the door for her, but really she shouldn't have been. Gabriel was hardly credible with his information and this was *Michaela*, her eldest sister. Of course she'd butt into the coffee date she had with her parents.

Cassandra's lungs stopped working—but at the same time, paradoxically, it was nearly a relief. Michaela would certainly *emote*, at the least, and certainly bring the subject up if the three of them managed to chit-chat blandly for hours without doing it.

"Hello, Michaela," Cassie said, keeping her voice even. "I didn't know you'd be here."

"Of course you didn't," she answered coolly. "Do come in. The coffee's just been made."

She walked in. The house was pristine, as if it hadn't housed *nine people* yesterday presumably in a party. Their parents were sitting on their vast couch, already holding their cups of coffee—they set them down and stood up when Cassandra approached.

She accepted her mother's kiss and her father's hug as blandly as they'd given them and sat by them. Michaela chose an armchair to the side and crossed her legs, leaning back. Overall she gave the impression of someone who was there to watch the circus burn—which was funny to Cassandra, considering she knew Mike wouldn't be able to contain herself from butting into the conversation.

"Hello, Mom, Dad," Cassie said. "I hope you've slept well."

"There's no place like home," her father said. "I slept better even tired and jetlagged than in any of the hotels we visited in Italy."

Ah, so that was where they'd been.

"Mike of course prepared everything for us," her mother added, sending Michaela a smile. She hadn't really looked at Cassandra yet. "So we just got into bed without any of that pesky business of changing sheets and whatnot. Helen, the housekeeper, made us a wonderful breakfast, too."

"I'm glad," Cassandra said.

She got her own cup from the coffee table and brought it closer to herself. It smelled wonderful, because of course it did. She stirred in the sugar and felt her shoulders drawing in under the weight of the silence.

It stretched on. Cassie looked up from her coffee and her parents were trading looks she couldn't decipher, while Michaela was turned to Cassie with her eyebrows lifted as if to say, "And?"

Cassandra thought about her lovely Diana waiting for her one floor down and was suddenly absolutely done.

Diana was right. She had nothing to fear.

"Do you remember the Kress family?" she asked a bit too loudly. Her parents turned to her, surprised. "They used to be our neighbors before we moved out here. Diana—Lady Di—was my best friend. But you had a fight with her parents and moved us all out and cut all contact between me and her."

"I remember that vaguely," Michaela commented.

Diana didn't look away from her mother.

"Yes, I remember them," she answered after a beat. "Their mother was friends with our old housekeeper. What about them?"

They hadn't even noticed Cassandra had said she was dating Diana, yesterday. Her fingers tightened against her cup for a second before she relaxed.

"*Why?*" she asked, keeping her voice as level as she could. "What did you fight about? Why did we move out—what happened that was so bad you had to remove me completely from Diana's family?"

Why did you do this to me, she thought as she had the last fourteen years. She could have been so, so much less lonely.

"Oh, that was nothing," she answered, waving a hand. "Mrs. Kress came to confront us about our parenting, out of everything, which was less than pleasant—"

"But we didn't move out because of that," her father completed, shaking his head as if Diana had asked a stupid question. "We'd been planning the move already—and that girl wasn't good for you. She was distracting you from your studies and from your family, so it wasn't much for us to block their phones so you wouldn't see her anymore."

Cassandra stared at them.

"It wasn't much," she parroted, hollow.

She thought about all those years, lost.

She thought of how much it'd *hurt* when she'd realized her parents had blocked her from her best friend, from *her* parents, who actually cared about Cassandra; she thought about all the days, weeks, *months* she spent devising plans to try and talk to Diana, foiled every time by her parents or her older siblings or the new housekeeper. She remembered all the nights she'd cried, how *lonely* she felt, how it took her *years* to give up hope that she'd see Diana again.

Why did you do this to me? It was a question Cassandra's had wanted to ask for over a decade now. She'd just been a kid, awkward and lonely, and they took her only friend.

Why?

Oh, that was nothing, her mother answered.

Cassandra stood up, furious tears in her eyes.

"I didn't think I could be more disappointed in you," she said, voice dripping with anger. Her tears slid down her cheeks. "Mrs. Kress was right. *You did wrong by me.* By all of us. You're incapable of having the littlest meaningful conversation with me and I'm sick of it. Thank you for the financial help all these years. That was all you were ever good for."

Michaela stood up, a frown on her face as angry as Cassandra's—and Cassie saw on her sister's face a kind of desperation, some hint of regret in the way she glanced at their stunned parents.

Of course it'd been Michaela. When did anyone else in their family even do *anything* without her?

"Were you the one who set this up?" she asked, voice wobbly.

"This conversation needs to happen," Michaela said, straightening up. She glanced at their parents again, but they weren't saying anything. They weren't going to. "Our family has an *image*—the company has an image—and you just can't go around kissing a *woman*, Cassandra. People will see and it will hurt us. I've nothing against you *personally* having that…inclination, but—"

Cassie laughed. Michaela's mouth closed shut.

"Mike," she told her stunned sister, "I don't *care*. I quit. And—you know, you may be arrogant and rude, but at least you care. Thank you for that."

She turned to her parents.

They really weren't going to say anything, but maybe that was just fine.

"Bye," she said. "I'll be very happy when I'm out of here. I hope that makes you at least a little bit happy, too."

She got her purse from the couch and left.

***

She went down to her own apartment and crowded Diana against the door. She kissed, kissed, and kissed her deeply. For once in her life she felt *all right.*

Chapter Fifteen

It was a hassle to take all of Cassie's clothes, bedclothes, blankets, pillows, boxes of make-up, and books to Diana's tiny apartment, and she certainly didn't have the space to house it all. A lot of it Isabella ended up taking to her house to store it until Cassie decided what she wanted to do with it, and with her help the three of them managed to get Cassie settled in Di's apartment with only a few trips.

Diana kissed Cassie on their lumpy couch and wondered if it was too soon, too sudden, too rash—but Cassie couldn't stop laughing in between her bouts of crying, so maybe that was fine. They'd figure it out together, once Cassie calmed down some.

They threw all of Cassie's pillows on Diana's bed and slept on a nest.

***

"So she's just… moved in?" Manuela asked, with a slightly judging tone.

"Hey, what was she supposed to do?" Diana asked, wrestling her phone, two sweaters, and three dirty plates between her two hands. "After that scene at her parents' apartment, she couldn't damn well *stay*."

"So now she's living with *you*. In our tiny cramped apartment."

"Aw, don't worry," Diana soothed. "I didn't give her your old room, it's still just as you left it."

"I'm rolling my eyes," Manuela said, amused. "Fine, what now? She's moved out, she quit—"

"Right *now*," Diana said, checking the hour on her microwave's display, "she's going to meet Jimmy once he arrives in about five seconds, and that's about as far into the future we're planning."

"That doesn't sound very responsible."

"Hey, this all went down *yesterday.* Don't judge. I'm giving her some time."

"Fine, fine, I'm not judging!" Manny lied. "I wish I was there to see her meeting Jimmy. Actually, I wish I was there to meet her! I haven't yet. You need to bring her next time you visit."

Diana grinned to herself.

"Sure. I'll—"

"*Di!*" Carl shouted from downstairs. "*Jim's here!*"

"*Okay!*" she shouted back.

She set the plates by the sink then threw the sweaters at the hamper in the corner of the kitchen. She skipped down the stairs and crashed into Jimmy, who caught her in a tight hug. Di relaxed into his hug, feeling stress rolling off her back and disappearing.

"Hey, girl," he said, patting her shoulder. "Been some time, huh?"

"Far too long," she said, shaking her head, then leaned away. "Come on, old man, give me all these groceries and let's go up. I've someone I want you to meet."

***

Jimmy walked in and immediately squinted around, suspicious. Diana put his many groceries on top of the counters and tried to hastily wash the last plates she'd dropped into the sink a second ago while he went peering around the room.

143

"This place is cleaner," he declared after a moment.

"The surprise in your voice wounds me," Diana said.

"I'm glad you've a girl to clean around now," he continued as if she hadn't said anything. "This place needed a woman's touch."

"Hey!"

"Diana. Remember the *molding box of pizza* I found in the corner of your *room* a few months ago? I remember. I have nightmares about it."

"Whatever," she muttered. She dried her hands. "Come on, Jimmy, what did you bring? What're you going to make?"

"What, you're putting me to work already? I thought I was meeting your Cassandra!"

"Hello," Cassie said, awkward, lingering at the door of the bedroom like she didn't quite have the courage to step out.

"There you are," Jimmy said warmly. It was enough for Cassie to step out and accept a handshake. "It's so, so nice to meet you, *finally*. This one..." he said pointing to Di, "hasn't shut up about you for a damn *lifetime* now."

"I see," Cassandra said, glancing at Diana as if asking for help.

"That's my Cassie," Diana said fondly. "She lives here now, you know?"

"*What?*" Jimmy asked, startled.

Diana shook her head.

"Come on, old man, put a cake in this oven and I'll explain to you what's been going on."

***

"And then she said *what?*" Jimmy asked, shoveling some cake into his mouth. It was fine, since it was a zero sugar cake he'd just popped into the oven to heat it up a bit.

"She said the family and the company had images and I couldn't just go around kissing a woman," Cassie told him. Her face was flushed, her eyes bright—she seemed *so happy* with Jimmy's hovering, grandfatherly attention. Diana really should have introduced them before.

"That's some bullshit right there," Jimmy said gruffly, shaking his head.

"*Bullshit* is the perfect word for all that," Diana agreed with a nod.

"Can't believe she could say that to her *baby sister*," Jimmy kept on, eating more cake. "I mean, look at you, Diana! You treated Manuela like she was a precious toddler up until she moved out! And you're still so good with her. I can't even imagine you doing something like this."

"I would *never!*"

"I'm glad," Cassandra said softly. She sent Diana a small smile.

"Well, I hope you can repair your relationship with them. God knows how we all are with family… can't escape them," Jimmy said.

Cassie looked down.

"I hope so too," she said.

"So, Jimmy," Diana said, setting her plate on top of her coffee table. "I actually had something to tell you, and since we're sitting here chatting, I might as well say it now."

"Oh, boy," Jimmy said, looking at the ceiling as if asking for help.

She took his plate from him and put it on top of hers and Cassie stood up to take them to the kitchen—to give them a moment with some kind of privacy. Diana caught Jimmy's hands in hers. They were rough and fat, the hands of a grandpa.

"So, you know the college fund?" she asked. He nodded, still looking apprehensive. "Manuela is right. She's an adult and of course I should help her, but this fund isn't necessary. She's not twelve anymore."

"Oh, thank God," Jimmy said with a sigh. "*Please* tell me you're changing your shower head."

"Eventually," Diana said dryly. "What I meant is—I know you've been having issues with money for all your expensive medicine and all the exams you have to do and that your kids aren't miracle workers and can't create money out of nowhere. Well, now I've got enough money to help."

"Oh," Jimmy said, squeezing her hands with a frown on his face. "Oh, no, Diana. I told you that I've—"

She shook her head.

"I'm also not a charity case," he told her, lifting his eyebrows. "We'll figure it out."

"You told me I was family, too."

He blinked at her. "Of course, Diana. What's that got to do with this? I'm not taking your money from you."

"Your kids are doing their best to help you, aren't they?" she asked. She looked at him in the eyes. They were hard to see from under his impressive eyebrows and behind his glasses, but they were the most beautiful blue she'd ever seen. "If I'm your family, I should do my best to help you too. You need it more than Manny anyway."

He shook his head.

"Jimmy, come on," she said before he could say anything. "You need your meds, don't fight me on this."

"Oh," he said, deflating. He wiped a hand over his eye. "Diana, I watched you struggle so much those first few years, I—"

"Aw, you old man," she said, and pulled him into a hug. He enveloped her into his arms. "Haha, do you think your kids are going to let you visit more often? I mean, they *gotta*, right?"

"Oh, so that's what this is about," Jimmy joked, shaking his head. "Diana, you idiot. They're going to cry, and probably officially adopt you. They've been— everybody's been so stressed about this, girl, you don't even *know*—"

"Because you kept avoiding the subject—"

"—but you gotta expect an invitation to Sunday lunch next week, Lady Di. That's how it's gonna be from now on."

"Christ, finally," Diana said, throwing her hands up. "I've been trying to get your family to adopt me for *years.* Hey, Cassie!" she called to the kitchen.

"We'll probably be able to celebrate Christmas with a proper family this year! Imagine that."

"Imagine that," Cassie repeated, amused.

***

Di and Cassie fell into bed together, tired after a day of cooking and laughing. Cassie was wearing one of Diana's shirts and Di was wearing the sweater she'd pilfered from Cassie that time she'd taken a bath at her apartment.

Di hugged Cassie to her chest even though she was shorter and Cassie curled up around her under the blankets.

"I totally support your decisions," Diana murmured, carding her fingers through Cassandra's beautiful hair. "But I can't believe you're really letting Isabella's friend chop it all off in a couple of days."

Cassie laughed a breathy laugh.

"It can grow back," she reassured.

"You've just started letting it down around me! So unfair."

"You should grow *yours* out," Cassie retorted. "I love it, but it's kind of a weird length right now."

"Eh, that's what happens when you shave your head and then do nothing for about five months after."

"Wow."

"Yeah."

"Gabe sent me a few texts," Cassie whispered. "He wants to have lunch somewhen. I don't know. He was always just rude and kind of clueless, but…"

"Yeah. I mean, what's the harm in going?" Diana asked.

Cassie laughed. "You're right. What's the harm, right? I spent so long doing absolutely nothing at all. Why not go to lunch with my brother?"

"Yeah. Speaking of brothers—Manny wants to meet you. She really doesn't remember you at all."

"What a travesty. When's the next trip scheduled? I can go anywhere, since I'm unemployed now."

"Eh, we haven't settled on it yet. She was going to come here, but I think it's kind of cramped now."

"Hm."

"Hey, Cassie," Di whispered. "I love you."

Cassie flushed, pleased.

"I love you too," she murmured back. "And I also love the new fridge we're picking up next week."

"You just had to ruin the moment."

www.ingramcontent.com/pod-product-compliance
Lightning Source LLC
Chambersburg PA
CBHW052355060726
47592CB00020B/2445